THE VENTILATED HEAD

A pop singer, an explosive bombshell of a girl, and her hippy boyfriend. A combination like that could go any-where — or thought they could. When Matt Grant became a big time pop singer money came and went, but it went faster than it came. When the inevitable crash came, Matt worked as a door-to-door salesman — and met Lindsay. And it was then Matt found that the life of an out-of-work pop singer was more than hard — it was murder.

Books by Anthony Nuttall
in the Linford Mystery Library:

THE CHINESE DOLL AFFAIR

ANTHONY NUTTALL

THE VENTILATED HEAD

Complete and Unabridged

LINFORD
Leicester

First published in Great Britain by
Robert Hale Limited
London

First Linford Edition
published 2006
by arrangement with
Robert Hale Limited
London

British Library CIP Data

Nuttall, Anthony
    The ventilated head.—Large print ed.—
Linford mystery library
1. Detective and mystery stories
2. Large type books
I. Title
823.9'14 [F]

ISBN 1–84617–297–7

Published by
F. A. Thorpe (Publishing)
Anstey, Leicestershire

Set by Words & Graphics Ltd.
Anstey, Leicestershire
Printed and bound in Great Britain by
T. J. International Ltd., Padstow, Cornwall

This book is printed on acid-free paper

1

She was small, but not smaller than I like women. She was young enough to be very attractive, but old enough to be interesting. Her figure had curves in all the right places, and there was an elfin touch about her face which would have brought it just to the human side of a chocolate box prettiness. But for her eyes. They were hard, flat, black. Looking into them was like peering into two holes drilled into a football, because there was exactly the same feeling of utter emptiness, the impression that nothing was there. No feeling, no warmth, and certainly none of the kindness and sympathy that a girl might have been expected to show towards a man who was ill in bed.

Or at least, in bed.

I didn't actually feel unwell, but I had the feeling that until recently I'd been ill. I frowned, trying to puzzle it out, but everything was covered with a gentle

1

vagueness, like one of those light mists which you sometimes see over the fields early on a summer morning, and which swirl and wreath, giving an occasional glimpse, an impression that there's something beyond, even if you can't make out any of the details.

Mist, hell.

It was more like a thick fog, because I hadn't the slightest idea what I was doing in bed, or who the girl was. All I knew was my name.

Matt Grant.

I turned it over and over in my mind. I thought it was a good name, and I was sure it belonged to me, for there was a basic understanding about it as if it was so deeply rooted in my mind that I couldn't forget it, whatever happened.

And something had happened. Even though I now knew nothing about it something drastic must have gone on in the past to put me in this bed. I turned it over and over in my mind but it didn't get me anywhere. For all I knew I could have been a robot from which someone had carelessly left out the memory bank.

So I lay in the bed and stared at the girl, until eventually she turned away.

'What's the matter?' she asked irritably. 'Have you got nothing better to do than lie there, staring?'

'I don't know,' I replied. 'I haven't the faintest idea what I've got to do.'

'Then you'd better get to know.' Her voice hardened. 'I've got better things to do than nurse you all the time, and it's about time you knew it.'

I put my head on one side and looked at her again, hitching myself up on the crumpled pillow to get a better view. She was still turned away, standing near the dressing table and looking towards the window, stopping me from seeing her face. Faded blue curtains were drawn over the window, and the room was lit by a single bulb which poked queerly out of a shade which was far too small for it. Where she was standing threw her into the shadows, but even so, she didn't look like a nurse.

Not even to my cottonwool mind.

She hadn't the expression of a nurse, or the attitude, and in any case I've never seen a nurse on duty in a shiny leather skirt, a pale green blouse and a black leather waistcoat jacket which looked like something Wyatt Earp might have thrown off in his youth.

Nor did the room look as though it was in a hospital.

It was too scruffy for that. Faded wallpaper. Battered furniture, even dingier than the stuff you find in the average hospital. Dirt in the corners, clearly visible in the stark light from the bulb. A tattered square of carpet on the floor with the remains of what had once been a cheerful pattern on it. A one bar electric fire, glowing brightly in the old-fashioned grate, the hard black line of the cable snaking across the carpet to a plug in the corner.

It couldn't have been a room in a hospital, yet there didn't seem anything else it could be.

I grinned.

The girl turned to look at me.

'What are you laughing at?' she asked in a bored voice.

'I'm not laughing, I'm getting ready to

ask the classic question.' I paused. 'Where am I?'

She frowned.

'Don't try that,' she said.

'I'm not trying anything. I just want to know where I am.'

'You must think I'm stupid or something.' She swung round from the window, her elbow catching the edge of one of the curtains, making it quiver. 'Don't think you can take me in like that.'

'I'm not trying to take anyone in.'

'You needn't waste your time.' There was an undercurrent of anxiety to her voice and I shook my head, wishing that I could dredge up something other than the awful emptiness which was all that remained of my mind. Maybe there was a simple explanation to all this, but in that case why didn't the girl tell me? And if she wasn't a nurse, who was she? And what was this place?

I moved, and the bed creaked. I decided to test her out a little and see what came of it.

'Look, nurse — '

'I'm not a damned nurse!' she snapped

at once. 'Nobby might think I am but the sooner we can get rid of you the better I'm going to like it.'

All right, so she wasn't a nurse. At least I'd found out something, though whatever her feelings about me might be there was a curiously final ring about the idea of getting rid of me which did me no good at all.

'If you don't want to be called nurse you'd better tell me your name,' I suggested.

'What does it matter to you?'

'It doesn't matter anything to me. I just thought it might be more friendly, that's all. Pardon me if I was wrong.'

'I should save your breath,' she said. 'You'll want it all for when Nobby comes to talk to you.'

'Maybe he'll turn out to be more civil than you are. Do you think he might even answer my question and tell me where I am?'

She laughed.

'I don't know about answering your questions. It's going to be Nobby who asks the questions, and whatever you're

6

trying to pretend with me won't work with him. He's not stupid, you know.'

'I never said he was. All I suggested was that he might be more civil.'

Again that short laugh which I was starting to dislike so much.

'You don't know Nobby,' she said. 'Whatever else you might call him, he isn't civil. Sometimes I wonder why I ever tied up with him, then at times like this I think I did the right thing after all.'

As she was speaking she crossed to the wall and yanked out the plug of the fire. The glowing bar began to fade.

'Where is this Nobby?' I asked. 'How about a word with him, or is that too much to ask?'

'You'll be having a word with him later on today.'

'That's great,' I said. 'Maybe I'll get some sense out of him.'

'And maybe he'll get some out of you.'

With that crack she opened the door and went out, banging it after her. A moment or two later I heard her footsteps as she started to go down some stairs.

I lay in bed, staring at the closed door,

wondering what was going on. Even without the fire the room didn't seem cold, but when I tried to remember getting there, or to think of a time when I hadn't been in the room, there was nothing. It was like looking down a deep mine shaft. There must be something at the bottom, that was only common sense, but the darkness hid it and meant that it would never be seen.

Unless I actually fell down the shaft.

After a while, in desperation, I tried that, picturing the blackness as a hole in the ground and imagining myself standing on the edge. I tried to jump down it, but it didn't work; evenually, feeling like some kind of nut, I gave up and simply stared at the ceiling.

Could be that's what I was. A nut. Would that account for my not being able to remember anything? Probably not and in any case it didn't add up; I could remember everything that had happened since I'd opened my eyes, everything that the girl had said, every detail of her appearance.

Yet before that, nothing.

Gradually it dawned on me that the girl, whoever she was, must know how I came to be here, what I was doing, what she was doing. Somewhere in that girl's mind was the answer to everything I wanted to know, and I'd just lay in the bed and let her fob me off with a lot of nonsense about someone called Nobby who was going to come and get me to answer his questions.

He'd be lucky. I couldn't even answer my own, let alone anyone else's. But if that girl could answer mine then she was going to and this time I wasn't going to be brushed aside by any off-hand remarks.

Throwing back the bedclothes I sat up and swung my feet over the side. I was wearing a pair of red and green striped pyjamas which were slightly too big for me, and apart from that weren't the kind of thing that I'd buy. I could remember nothing about where they'd come from, but that didn't surprise me. I stood up and the chill of the cracked lino which covered the parts of the floor that the carpet didn't reach struck through my bare feet.

Determinedly I set off towards the square of carpet, halfway to the door.

I never got there.

When I was a couple of feet away from the bed the dizzy feeling started. At first I took no notice but shuffled on; within a few seconds I had spiralled to such an extent that I had to take notice. The beginnings of a cry jerked out of my mouth but were cut off almost at once as I hit the floor. The carpet felt rough and coarse between my fingers, and a dull ache, as if two or three little men with knives were starting work, began to spread at the front of my head. I tried to shout again but only managed a croak. Lights seemed to be flashing on and off all around me, but there wasn't the slightest sound anywhere.

Slowly the lights faded. The dull ache was still there, stretching in a band across the front of my head, but even that seemed slightly less intense than it had done before, as if a couple of the men had given up and gone home, leaving just one to work overtime.

After what seemed a good few hours I managed to stand up. The room was still swaying slightly, but not so much that I couldn't cope with it. Hoping that it might go off completely I stayed where I was, but when it didn't I decided to try and get to the door anyway.

Moving might do me some good. Or it might not.

Oddly enough, it did. After I'd taken a few steps I felt a lot better, and by the time I was at the door I was striding out like a soldier on the march. Confidently I reached out to turn the handle. Nothing happened. Tightening my grip I tried again, turning more and more violently, until I was rattling it in a savage fury. I didn't do the slightest good. That door was locked, and it was staying that way.

'Hey!' I yelled, hoping that the girl would hear, but all I got back was the echo of my own voice from the fading wallpaper.

'Open this door!' I cried, rattling the handle again, without having any effect.

There was no sign of the girl either.

Presently it filtered through to my brain

that there was nothing else for it but to go back to bed. Without the stimulation of the feeling that I might soon have a solution to the mystery I was starting to feel the cold, too, and I shivered a little. My head was still aching, but it was nothing compared to the way in which my brain throbbed as I tried to figure out what was going on.

The trouble was that there was nothing to give me a clue.

Not even any of my clothes. I made that discovery a few minutes later when I opened the door of the wardrobe which was pushed against the wall, opposite the door. It was empty, apart from a newspaper. I took it out and brushed off the dirt. The date meant nothing to me, and I turned the pages over quickly, picking out the main news stories, anxious to find out whether or not I could remember them.

I couldn't.

Somehow, the discovery was the worst one I'd made yet, even worse than finding out that the door was locked. That all the things in that newspaper should have been going on, and for all the impression they had made on me they might never have happened. For all the sense they made I might have been a visitor from space who'd bought a late edition paper just to pick up the threads of life on earth and who had found it more complicated than he'd realized.

Only the name of the paper was familiar.

Vaguely I knew that it had been around for a long time, that one of the things which had happened before I had opened my eyes to see the girl, one of the continuing events in the black tunnel of memories which was all I had, was that a newspaper called the *Daily Express* had been published.

The memory didn't help me at all. I flung the paper back where I'd found it, then closed the wardrobe door and went over to the window.

As soon as I pulled back the curtain I saw at once that there was no way out there. The room I was in appeared to be near the top of one of those big, old houses that are usually converted into flats these days. I assumed that whoever owned this one had the full use of it, which was why they were able to keep me here. As far as I could make out there was nothing which would help me to get down the wall if I climbed out of the window; the only drainpipes were much too far away to be of any use to me.

I tried opening the window, but it was firmly closed, and when I looked more closely I spotted the bright heads of new nails, all round the frame, where it had recently been nailed up.

Specially for me? They needn't have bothered.

Pulling the curtains closed again I turned back to the room, still staggering a little but much better now than I had been.

One of the other things I was wondering was how long I'd been a prisoner. When I ran my hand over my chin I could feel the stubble and hear it rasping; from that I guessed that it was no more than a couple of days.

Had I been lying in the bed all that time? I must have been unless the memory block was only recent. For all I knew I could have been walking around normally an hour or so ago, and have no memory of it now. Sitting on the edge of the bed I tried to think back, tried to work out what had led up to this situation, but there was nothing other than the blackness which I already knew so well.

With a sigh I got back into bed and pulled the covers round me. I might as well keep warm while I waited for Nobby to put in an appearance.

*   *   *

He came later. Much later. As I had no watch, or any means of telling the time I can't be certain how long I waited for him, and I may even have fallen asleep in the meantime. Somehow, everything seemed hazy, but at least I could remember talking to the girl, the way I'd prowled around the room after collapsing, and the man's name.

Nobby.

He came up the stairs so quietly that

when he opened the door I was taken by surprise. He was both bigger and younger than I'd expected, though in spite of his size he wasn't running to fat. Not yet anyway. He stood in the doorway, his hands on the doorposts as if he was trying to push them further apart to make sure he could squeeze through, and while he looked at me, I looked at him.

A red face, as if he'd been playing football in the cold all morning. A blue pullover. Grey casual trousers. Quite smart, really, if you discounted the expression on his face. A snarling, ferocious expression, as if his sole thought while he'd been playing football had been what he was going to do to me when the game was over.

After a moment or two he stepped right into the room, and I saw then that with him was a little fellow. He had the kind of scared look on his face that I felt I ought to be wearing, and in his hand he was carrying a black leather doctor bag. He had on an overcoat, too, so he'd obviously come in from outside. On his head was a bowler hat. Him and the big bloke together looked like a pair of third-rate comedians trying to take-off Laurel and Hardy and not quite making it.

'He's come round,' the thin one said in a reedy voice which I could soon get to dislike.

'I told you he had,' Nobby replied irritably. 'You'd better get on with it, hadn't you?'

The thin man nodded, but as he scurried round the side of bed I put up my hand and he stopped, looking uncertainly from me to Nobby.

'Just a minute,' I said mildly. 'Before either of you gets on with anything, how about telling me what's going on?' As I said that I remembered what the girl had said about Nobby not being civil, and I waited to see what his reaction to the question would be.

She was right.

'Shut your face, punk,' he said to me. 'Let the doc have a look at you.'

Doctor? I didn't need a doctor. I started to tell them so, then caught a glimpse of the expression on Nobby's face and thought better of it. After all, if I

17

couldn't recall anything that had happened prior to a few hours ago, maybe I did need a doctor.

The thin man was fishing in his bag. He had all the gear in there, and made a quick examination. So far as I could judge he was competent, but his face had that neutral expression which all doctors use, so that you can't tell whether you're bursting with health or likely to be dead within the hour. Eventually he stepped back, smiling, and unhooked his stethoscope.

'This man's as fit as I am, Nobby,' he said.

Looking at his thin, scrawny neck and arms and his pinched face I couldn't decide whether or not that was a desirable state of affairs, but there was one point on which he needed putting right.

'I've lost my memory,' I said.

'There's nothing the matter with you,' he said, still smiling. 'I'm the doctor round here.'

'And I'm me,' I said. 'I ought to know whether or not I can remember anything.'

'You might be putting it on,' Nobby

said. 'An act, like. Trying to fool Doctor Kyme and me.'

'That's true,' Kyme agreed. 'Don't worry about that, Nobby, because if he is he'll slip up sooner or later.'

'Look — '

'I've already told you once,' Nobby snarled. 'Shut up until I start asking you questions. Sally said that you talked too much and she was right.'

Sally must be the girl I'd seen earlier. That was one thing I was going to remember. In the meantime there were other complications, and I turned to Kyme.

'You're a doctor,' I said to him. 'You ought to be able to tell whether or not I've really lost my memory or whether I'm putting it on.'

He shook his head. The light from the badly shaded bulb glinted on his bowler hat.

'I can't tell for sure. No one can. In your case I'd say that you were putting it on, and if I was in the position you're in I'd do the same. Don't think that it'll do you any good, though.'

'Suppose you get someone here who knows what he's talking about,' I suggested. 'That way we might all get somewhere.'

'You'll get somewhere in a minute,' Nobby said, 'but it won't be where you expect. Just shut your face while I have a talk to the doc.'

They moved away to a spot near the door, looking just like one of those serious huddles of consultants and doctors that you get in all the best hospitals. Only this wasn't a hospital, and I could see no good coming out of it as far I was concerned. There didn't seem anything I could do about it while I was still in the bed, and with a quick gesture I flung back the clothes. In spite of my memory I hadn't forgotten what had happened last time I'd got up, and if it happened now it might at least convince Kyme that everything wasn't as well as he thought.

I stood up.

This time nothing happened.

The room didn't whirl round, I didn't collapse, there were no funny feelings at all. I walked over to where Nobby and the doctor were talking and just as I reached them Nobby turned round.

'The punk's out of bed!' he exclaimed, a light springing into his eyes. 'Is that safe for him, doc?'

Kyme giggled. It was a thin shrilling sound, like a knife being rubbed over glass, that did me no good at all. There was an odd look in his eyes, too, that combined with the giggle to change him from a semi-comic figure into something quite different. Something dangerous and menacing, and something which, in spite of the difference in their sizes, was more to be feared than Nobby.

I stopped in my tracks and looked at him warily.

'It isn't safe for him to be out of bed, Nobby,' he said. 'From the expression on your face I'd say it was the most unsafe thing he could have done.' Again there was that dreadful sound from his mouth. 'You'll have to do better than this if you want to be a nurse.'

'I don't want to be a goddamned nurse!' he cried. 'Though Grant will need one when I'm through.'

He took a step towards me. I stayed right where I was, waiting for him.

'Back to bed, Grant,' he said, like a father with a small child.

I shook my head.

'The doc says there's nothing wrong with me. Unless you can give me a good reason why I should do what you say I'm getting out of here. What you'd better do is get me my clothes.'

He raised his eyebrows.

'I thought you'd lost your memory?'

'I have.'

'Then it isn't safe for you to be wandering the streets, is it? I'm doing you a kindness, keeping you here.'

'I'd rather be in a proper hospital,' I said, raising my voice so that it could be heard above the shrilling giggles of the man who called himself the doctor. 'I don't think the kind of treatment I'm getting here is helping me at all.'

Nobby didn't speak. He stepped forward a pace and got hold of my arm. I tried to shake him off, but I might as well have tried to push over Marble Arch. I tried again, but before I could make any impression on him he grabbed my other arm and actually picked me off the ground.

'Get back into bed, punk!' he hissed into my face, then thrust me away from him. Unable to help myself I staggered backwards until I hit the bed and fell onto it.

'He won't forget that,' Kyme said.

'I'll give him a lot of other things he won't forget if he doesn't watch himself,' Nobby said, glowering at me and flexing his fingers.

I ran my tongue over my lips. Maybe I should have got up again and had another go at him but somehow I didn't feel up to it. The discovery that there was no more strength in my arms than there was in a couple of rotten twigs had frightened me far more than he had done, and rather than risk any more trouble I did as he said.

'Sure you can manage him, Nobby?' the doctor said.

'I'll manage him. Don't worry about that.' Abruptly Nobby laughed, a hearty guffaw that was a refreshing contrast to the doctor's giggling. Kyme put his hand on Nobby's arm, nodding his head, then they both went to the door. I watched them, and wasn't surprised when Nobby paused at it.

'You'd better go down on your own, doc,' he said. 'Grant and I have urgent things to talk about. Sally will fix you up.'

Kyme nodded and clattered away down the stairs, the sound vanishing as soon as Nobby closed the door again.

'Well?' he said, coming to stand at the side of the bed and looking down at me.

'Well, what?' There was irritation in my voice. 'Maybe if someone would tell me what was going on — '

'You don't need any telling what's going on,' Nobby declared. 'You heard what the doc said. You're as fit as he is.'

'From looking at him I don't know if that's a good thing or a bad one,' I said, 'but it still doesn't alter the fact that I don't know what's going on.'

Nobby didn't make any reply to that. Turning, he grabbed the wooden chair which was next to the wardrobe and brought it over to the bed. He placed it neatly a few inches from the side of the bed, shifting it a little until he was satisfied that it was exactly where he wanted it, then he sat down. He smiled at me, his teeth flashing white in his red face. He looked like Father Christmas in the off-season.

'Listen, punk,' he said, completely destroying the image, 'you know what's going on as well as I do. Suppose you tell me.'

'If you know it so well, what's the point in my telling you?' I grinned back at him.

'There are some bits that I don't know and you do,' Nobby said gently. 'They're the most important bits. I want you to tell me about them.'

We were going round in circles and there didn't seem any way out. The main point was to convince him that I really had lost my memory; without that we were in one of those non-productive situations which can go on for a long time. I stared at him as he sat by the side of the bed, and then I shrugged.

'You can wait as long as you want,' I

said. 'It still won't alter the fact that I've lost my memory.'

'Kyme said — '

'I don't care what he said, it doesn't alter the facts. I can remember my name and the things that have happened in the past couple of hours but that's all.'

'What is your name?'

'Matt Grant.' I tried to say it confidently, but something about the way he'd asked the question threw doubts about even that into my mind. To my relief he nodded his head slowly.

'Can't quarrel with that,' he said. 'If you can remember your name how come you can't remember anything else?'

'How the hell should I know? That's something you should ask that doctor downstairs. Assuming that he is a doctor, of course.'

'He's a doctor all right,' Nobby said. 'You won't find him on any register, but he's a doctor.'

That was all I wanted. Being shut up with this goon and having a missing memory was bad enough. On top of it, I was being tended by a struck off doctor.

'Why did they strike him off?' I asked. 'Couldn't he tell whether or not a man had lost his memory?'

'That's enough of the smart talk,' Nobby said. 'You're trying, I'll say that for you, but it isn't going to work. I'll make sure of that.'

'I can't remember anything,' I said dully.

'Except your name,' he finished sneeringly. 'You'll have to do better than that, Grant. How about your address? Do you remember where you live?'

I shook my head. That was something which I hadn't considered up to now, that even if I got out of here I'd have nowhere to go. I presumed that I had a home somewhere but I didn't have the faintest clue where it was, or even if there was anyone else living with me who might be wondering what had happened to me.

Nobby pursed his lips.

'How about Lindsay?' he asked. 'Me and the boys could have fun with Lindsay if you didn't get your memory back and couldn't give me the answers to my questions.'

I shrugged.

'I don't know what you're talking about, so that line isn't going to work.'

He ran his tongue over his lips, staring at me, looking intently into my face as if that helped him to read what was going on inside my head. Finally he shook his head slowly and leaned back.

'We could have some real good fun with Lindsay.'

'Suit yourself,' I told him.

I was starting to rattle him, I could see. At first he had been confident that Kyme was right when he said that I was bluffing; now he wasn't sure. I felt sorry for the unknown Lindsay, of course, but she meant no more to me than the girl downstairs, Sally; less, actually, because at least I knew who Sally was and could remember what she looked like.

'Suppose we got Lindsay here,' Nobby said, with just a trace of uncertainty in his voice. 'What would you say to that?'

'If she could tell me something about what happened it would be a help,' I said.

He scratched his head. His lips jutted out. He looked like an exceptionally ugly plate-lipped negress.

'It won't work,' he said flatly.

I shrugged.

He sprang to his feet, kicked the chair away from him so that it crashed across the room, then before I had time to get out of the way he thumped me across the face with his open hand. My head felt as if it was spinning round on top of my neck and his face, inches from mine, seemed to grow and swell, the features distorting grotesquely, as if they were drawn on an inflating balloon.

'I can't remember anything!' I yelled at him. 'You're stupid if you can't see that I'm telling the truth! All I want to do is — '

He moved and I broke off, expecting him to hit me again. He didn't. Grabbing hold of the front of the pyjamas with both hands he pulled me up and held me so that I was half out of bed.

'Punk!' he yelled. 'You'll talk before I've finished with you! There's forty thousand quid missing and you're the only one who knows where it is!'

But it wasn't that which burst into my

head and made me sit up of my own accord. It was what he said next, spoken in a voice which was little more than a whisper.

'At least you ought to,' he hissed. 'You killed a man to get it. Don't try and tell me you've forgotten that!'

* * *

When Nobby had gone, locking the door after him, the room seemed very quiet. For a long time I lay exactly where he had left me, the bedclothes barely covering me, the grip of his bunched fingers still showing at the collar of the pyjamas. My eyes were closed, but there was no thought in my mind of trying to sleep. Neither were there any thoughts of what might happen to me in the future; I was too concerned with what had already happened for that, though I was no nearer to sorting it out.

'Killed a man?' I'd said to Nobby, breaking the intense silence after about twenty seconds. 'What the hell are you talking about?'

30

He'd given me a quizzical glance, still holding me.

'You're putting up a good show, Grant,' he'd said, 'but it isn't going to work with me. I'll break you down sooner or later. If I were you I'd make it sooner.'

'Can't you accept — '

'You'd be surprised at some of the things the doc's got in that case of his,' Nobby went on. 'Real dreamy things. Drugs, stuff like that. We'll soon settle your brain if that's what's wrong with you, though whether you'd be good for anything afterwards is another matter.'

He'd let me go as he'd said that and I'd fallen back on the pillow. I could imagine the doc pumping me full of stuff, his bowler hat still on his head. Probably he'd giggle as he did it, and somehow that would make it much worse. Yet that didn't help me. I still couldn't have told Nobby what he wanted to know, and as for killing a man . . .

'This character I'm supposed to have killed,' I'd said to him as he'd stared down at me, his red face blotched here and there with white. 'Who was he? Why am I supposed to have done it?'

Nobby had shrugged.

'I guess he must have got in your way. Why does a punk like you do anything?'

'What was his name?'

'Can't help you there, pal. You killed him. You ought to know who he was without me having to tell you.'

'I'd know it if I had killed him,' I'd said, 'but I can't remember anything about it. However blank my mind is I'm sure I wouldn't forget a thing like that.'

It was the worst thing I could have said, for Nobby nodded his head.

'Sure you'd remember it,' he'd agreed. 'And you did kill him, there's no doubt about that. That's what makes me so sure you're lying when you say you've lost your memory. No one forgets something like that, especially when there's forty thousand quid hidden away as well.'

'That's another thing,' I'd begun, but Nobby was standing up and moving towards the door.

'You'll remember soon enough when Kyme gets to work on you,' he said as he reached it. 'That's if you know what's good for you. I don't aim to stand here and argue with you for much longer.'

When Kyme gets to work on you. Those were the words which still stuck in my mind, long after he'd gone. I seemed to see, even with my closed eyes, the thin figure of the man with the bowler hat, the man whom I wouldn't find on any register of doctors, and who seemed so harmless until he giggled. Whatever my own condition was I was sure that there was some kind of mental illness with Kyme, and while I couldn't even begin to guess what techniques he would use to try and make me talk there was no doubt that Nobby had faith in him. And with forty thousand quid at stake there was plenty of stimulus for him to think of something.

Forty thousand quid.

And I couldn't recall a thing about it.

Yet, according to Nobby, I was the only one who knew where it was. There was a joke in that, if only I could think of it. After a moment I gave up trying and shuddered; the joke would be over soon enough when Kyme returned the following day, and I would do better by trying to think of some way out of the mess that I was in.

Not that any brilliant ideas came to my mind right away. For a start I didn't even know where I was. Assuming that I could open the locked door and get out of the house without being spotted, what did I do then? If I had really killed a man the police were sure to be on the lookout for me, and in the red and green striped pyjamas, which were the only clothes I had, I wouldn't be easy to miss.

Not only that, but I didn't even have anywhere to head for, nor could I think of anyone who might help me. Once I left here I would be completely on my own and for a while even the thought of Doctor Kyme was better than the near certainty of being pulled in by the cops for a crime about which I could remember nothing.

Only for a while, though.

After that, thoughts of Kyme began to loom larger, until the image of him which I had in my mind grew so that he became a superhuman figure, a giant of a man beside whom Nobby was a mere pygmy. Every so often I thought I could hear his horrible giggling laughter, and I had no trouble at all imagining him doing that while he filled me full of drugs which would leave me a wreck by the time he'd finished.

Always assuming that anything that happened afterwards would interest me, for I remembered what the girl, Sally, had said about getting rid of me.

Presumably the doc would have a hand in that, too.

A useful character to have around.

Gradually, in spite of the worries on my mind, I must have fallen alseep, for when I opened my eyes again the room was noticeably darker and I was hungry. I looked around, not quite clear where I was, then the memory of the last few hours returned, and I began to shiver. This time, the thought of Kyme coming put me into a panic. I opened my mouth to shout, decided that it would do no good, and closed it again. When I swallowed, my throat was parched.

I was going to have to get out of this house.

The only question was how to do it.

Just walking through the door, assuming that I could open it, would solve nothing; without really knowing who I was and what the story behind the dead man and the forty thousand pounds I could too easily get myself into trouble. Anyway, I had nowhere to go, and I couldn't even remember the name of anyone who might be friendly towards me.

The only way round all those things seemed to be to use the girl, Sally, and as I lay on that hard bed I began to plan how she might help me. I was sure that she had the answers to all my questions, and if I really had forty thousand pounds to bargain with I must be in a much stronger position that I'd realized.

If I tried and she wouldn't play I might finish up worse off than I was now, but that was something I'd have to risk.

Eager now, I began to listen for footfalls on the stairs. There was only silence. I had no watch on, and I didn't know how long I'd been lying there when I heard the tread of someone coming up the stairs. At first I was afraid that it might be Nobby, but as the sound drew nearer I realized it could only be the girl. Lying back against the pillow I listened to the turning of the key in the lock.

The door opened, and Sally looked in.

When she saw I was in bed she seemed satisfied and stepped right into the room, turning and locking the door behind her. She'd changed out of the skirt and cowboy waistcoat, and when the door was closed she slipped the key into the pocket of her jeans.

'Decided to remember yet?' she asked in a hard voice.

'That depends.' I looked at the tray she was carrying. On it was a plate of meat and potatoes, and a dish of congealed rice pudding. 'For me?'

She nodded and dumped the tray on the bed.

'There's tea after, if you want it.'

'Just like the Ritz,' I said jeeringly. 'I'll want it right enough.' I reached for the tray and pulled it towards me. 'You can stick the rice pudding but the rest of it doesn't look so bad.'

She flushed slightly.

'It should be all right. I made it.'

'Specially for me.' I kept the jeering note in my voice. 'I didn't know you cared.'

'I don't. Not about you, at any rate.'

'What do you care about?' I asked, as if I couldn't have guessed.

'The forty thousand quid.'

I began to eat, deliberately letting her wait for an answer to that. When I'd had a few mouthfuls and the initial pangs of hunger had gone off I said:

'I might have known that all you'd be interested in would be the money.'

'What do you mean?' Wariness jumped into her eyes for a moment, then vanished as she remembered that her side held all the aces. Or at least, so she thought.

'I mean what I say,' I told her. 'The question is, how far are you prepared to go to get the money?'

'What do you mean?'

'Is that all you can say?' I asked irritably. 'What the hell do you think I mean? Assuming that I tell you where the stuff is, what sort of share will Nobby give you?'

'I don't see what that's got to do with you.' She moved towards the window and stood with her back to the drawn curtains, scuffing the carpet with her toe. Suddenly she let the raised edge fall with a little slap and turned to me, making an impatient gesture.

'Get on with your tea,' she said, 'and then I can get out of here.'

'Suit yourself. Are you going to tell me how much or not?'

She shook her head.

'Fair enough,' I said with a shrug. 'I might have been going to offer you more but I can't improve on something when I don't know its value.'

I thought she was going to ask me once again what I meant, but she didn't. Another gleam flickered in her eyes, then vanished when she saw how closely I was watching her. She kicked the carpet again, then she swung round to face me, her lips pressed tightly together.

'I don't know what you're driving at,

but whatever it is, you're wasting your time,' she said tautly.

I laughed.

'Am I, Sally?' I said. 'Ten thousand pounds is a lot of money.'

'Ten thousand?' she said after a pause.

I nodded.

'Then you're admitting that you do know where the money is?'

That was the main snag of my scheme, but I could see no way round it if I was to persuade her to help me get away from this place. Rather than say anything definite I kept quiet, letting her assume from my silence that she was right. She took about half a minute to absorb the fact, then she laughed shakily.

'What do I have to do to earn this ten thousand?' she asked.

'What do you think?'

'Get you away from here.' Another laugh, shriller this time. 'Nobby would kill me if I was stupid enough to try anything like that.'

'Ten thousand pounds is a lot of money,' I reminded her. 'If you play your cards right afterwards he need never see you again.' I paused. 'How much did you say he was giving you?'

'We haven't talked about it.'

'I suppose you don't mention sordid things like money when you're together,' I agreed, finishing the last of the meat, pushing the plate away and sneering at the mess of rice pudding which was still lurking on the tray. 'From what I've seen of him he wouldn't give you ten thousand.'

I could see that she was coming round to my view, but that it was going to take time and patience, because of her worries as to what Nobby might do after. Time was the one thing I didn't have. The doctor was coming back by morning, and once he and Nobby started in earnest I might as well give up; I had to have an answer from her, and I wanted it fast.

If I'd had clothes and somewhere to go, and had known what had been going on during the past few days, I'd have been tempted to push her to one side and risk getting caught up with Nobby on the way out. As it was, I had to have some form of help, which was why I was going through all this rigmarole.

I waited for her to say something else, feeling myself tensing as the atmosphere in the room grew tauter.

She opened her mouth. It was impossible to tell from her expressionless eyes what she was going to say.

'What I think — ' she began slowly, then a sudden sound made us both whirl towards the door.

'Sally!'

'That's Nobby,' she said, a note of panic creeping into her voice. 'He's probably wondering what's taking me so long.'

'Let him wonder,' I said, with an indifference that I was far from feeling. 'Isn't ten thousand pounds more important to you than Nobby?'

She looked at me, running her tongue over her lips, and then nodded. The scared look was still in her eyes, though, and she kept darting quick glances towards the door, as if she expected Nobby to creep up the stairs and burst in unexpectedly. I could tell from the way she was behaving that if I was to hold her attention I would have to do something quickly; once she got out of this room and back to Nobby she would easily fall under his influence again and I would have lost everything that I'd just been working towards.

Worse, I would have lost even the chance of getting help from anyone.

'Ten thousand in cash,' I said. 'Small notes with no record of the numbers. Think what you could do with it.'

She was already thinking, judging by the expression on her pretty little face. In fact, I reckon she'd been thinking it all along, and the only question now was whether her greed would overcome her fear of Nobby.

'What would I have to do?' she demanded suddenly, hissing the words at me in an attempt to keep her voice down.

'Get me some clothes. Arrange for me to get out of here before morning. And tell me what's going on.'

As soon as I said that I realized that in my haste to get her to agree I'd made a fatal error, but by then it was too late. If I didn't already know what was going on, how could I offer her ten thousand pounds? By talking about the money I'd as good as admitted that I knew all about it, and that the loss of memory had been nothing but an act.

I could see from her face that she realized all this, and that I hadn't a hope now of getting her to help me.

She backed swiftly to the door, fumbling behind her for the handle, not taking her eyes off me.

'I don't like you,' she said, gabbling the words into a long string in her haste to get them out. 'There's something queer about you. I think I ought to get Nobby up here to sort it out.'

Once Nobby came I was really sunk. The way I felt now, I might be able to get the better of him, but only if I could surprise him. If he came in at that door now he could beat me to a pulp and I was so weak that I wouldn't have a chance of stopping him. If I was onto him before he knew I was there, one good blow from me in the right place would soon even up matters between us.

I was out of the bed before she had the

door open. I felt a little unsteady on my feet but by keeping moving I managed to overcome that.

Sally's eyes widened, then rounded into staring pits, the hardness sliding out of them, revealing her for the frightened girl that she was. I'd no time to worry about chivalry, or anything like that; she'd chosen to play it this way, so that now she'd lost out she was going to have to take the consequences. By the time I reached her, her throat was already swelling for a scream. I managed to cut off the sound before it could come out, and then all I had to do was hold her.

I might have been weak from lying in the bed, but not so weak that I couldn't handle a girl. Or so I thought. She might have looked thin but she had a tough, wiry strength, and it took me all my time to hold her.

'Sally!' I muttered into her ear. 'Shut up, or you'll have him here!'

There was no hope of that working, but I had to try it, to see if there was still a slight chance of bringing her onto my side. There wasn't. She was biting my fingers, and clawing at my face with her free hand. A particularly vicious swipe only just missed my eyes; I pulled my head back at the last moment, felt a sudden stinging pain, and then blood trickled down my face.

'Sally!' Nobby cried from downstairs.

She mumbled something, but because my hand was across her mouth he couldn't have heard it.

Twisting furiously, she almost managed to break away, but I was too quick for her, grabbing her other arm and twisting it close to the other so that I could hold them both with one hand. While I was doing that she managed to get out a faint choked cry, and I half-expected Nobby coming up anyway when he got no answer to his shouts.

There was a silence, broken only by the harsh sound of our breathing.

I blinked some of the blood out of my eyes.

Sally had gone limp. Suddenly, she sprang into life again, jerking away from me and breaking free. Before I could stop her she had the door open and was halfway through it. In another second she would have yelled for Nobby, but I managed to grab her again and yank her back inside. She was really frightened now, and fighting with a savage fury, doing her best to claw my face every time she managed to get her hands free, so that it was all I could do to hold her.

That was why I didn't want to have too much of a fight against Nobby. In my own mind, I knew that I could never hope to beat him. If I once let Sally get away and warn him what was going on I might as well give up, and forget all about getting out of this place.

I slapped her across the face. The sound was very loud to me but I didn't think that it would have carried outside the room. For a moment Sally paused, a look of shock coming across her face, then she flew at me again. I slapped her once more. She stumbled on the edge of the carpet, falling before I could grab her, her head cracking against the wall.

She lay so still that I thought she must be dead.

My breath came in shallow gasps, even though my chest was heaving, and I had the feeling that unless I could draw in more air I would suffocate. Resting my hands on the bed to steady myself I forced myself to breath slowly and deeply for a second or two, then turned round to have a look at Sally.

If she was dead, it was murder.

Though as I was already supposed to have killed one person, according to Nobby, maybe that didn't matter so much.

Even so, when I cautiously bent over her and found that she was still breathing I was almost as relieved as I would have been had I managed to get out of the house. With her off my mind I could turn my attention to that again, and the obvious fact that I was going to have to abandon any plan of sneaking away, with or without her help. Pretty soon, Nobby was going to want to know what was happening, and when he came I would really be in trouble. I had to do something before then, and I shook my head angrily, trying to clear it, trying to get some sort of idea into it.

The pyjamas flapped loosely around me.

Before I could do much, I would have to have some clothes. Shoes particularly. Even if I went out in the pyjamas I couldn't hope to get far in my bare feet.

I moved to the door. There was no sound from Nobby, but that didn't mean that he'd given up. From what I'd seen of him I'd hazard a guess that he wasn't the kind of guy who gave up, and I went warily, not knowing what he might be planning. Carefully I opened the door. There was no sign of him on the stairs, no sound in the house to suggest that there was anyone around other than me and the unconscious girl, and I stepped onto the landing, a draught striking chilly through the thin pyjamas.

I started to walk down the stairs, still moving very slowly, not knowing when a tread might creak and warn him that I was coming, and then I stopped, for I had heard something.

A sound. Nothing very obvious. Just a faint murmuring noise which slid quietly up the stairs until it reached me, then carried on past and was lost. The sort of noise which someone sneaking along the passage might make. I stopped, hesitating now, then made a sudden decision and turned round, hurrying back into the bedroom.

Sally was still unconscious.

I stared down at her. I'm not a big guy, but even so I wasn't certain whether or not the bulky sweater and jeans that she was wearing would fit me. It seemed the only way that I was going to get anything, though, as it was obvious now that Nobby's suspicions were aroused and I'd have the devil of a job taking him by surprise. In any case, his things would be far too big for me. It was a question of one or the other, and as the girl was here that made up my mind for me.

Working as quickly as I could I got the jeans off her and tried them on. As I'd thought, they were a little on the small side, but no worse than some of the things that you see people wearing. The sweater was much better; where it had been rather loose on her, it fitted me perfectly. All that I needed now were some shoes, and, if I could get one, an overcoat.

If. That was a big word, because Nobby stood in between them and me.

There was something oddly familiar about the sight of Sally in bra and panties, as if I'd seen it before. I stared down at her, certain that something was on the edge of my memory, but just as I tried to push it over the brink and maybe get somewhere I heard the noise again.

This time it seemed right outside the door.

I whirled, my mouth suddenly dry, all thought of Sally gone.

There was no doubt that Nobby was standing there, waiting for me to come out.

Quickly, I went over to the window. I'd already checked once but this time I had to make really certain that there was no way out. When I pulled back the curtain, I realized that I was going to have to rely on what I'd seen before, because it was pitch dark outside and there was no chance of my seeing anything. I let the curtain fall back and swung round again.

The door handle was turning slowly.

I padded across to the door and stood near it, where I would be out of sight when it opened. With any luck, the first thing that would catch his eye when he came in would be Sally, and he might be so distracted by the sight of her that I would be able to hit him before he realized what was happening.

Then again, he might be expecting it, and not be distracted at all.

The door opened. Nobby stepped in. He looked a lot bigger than I'd remembered him, and I suddenly felt that in the too small jeans, with my bare feet poking out of the bottoms, there was no chance of my beating him.

His eyes fell on Sally. He took another pace forward, staring at her as she sprawled on the floor, then he seemed to realize his own danger. As he started to turn I chopped down with the edge of my hand and caught him on the back of his neck, just like you see on the television. In my case it didn't work as well as it does then, but it gave me time to grab the chair from near the bed and slam it over his head. Even that didn't put him out completely, but I wasn't hanging around to finish the job.

Right now I had the advantage, and I intended to keep it.

As his hand flapped across the floor towards my ankle I skipped out of the way, throwing the chair towards him, and ran out of the door. I banged it shut. The key was still in the lock. Turning it, I tossed the key to the far side of the landing, then ran down the stairs.

The house was bigger than I'd thought, and for a second or two as I reached the foot of the stairs I was lost. Any way could have led to the front door, and taking the wrong one would have meant delay, or even capture again.

Once they had me back, they would make sure that I couldn't get out next time.

The thought made me shudder, and I pushed open a door and looked into what was obviously the living room. I was going to give it a miss, as I obviously couldn't get out there, when a thought came into my mind, and I pushed the door open wider. The carpet tickled my bare feet as I padded across it, my eyes flickering round as I tried to find what I wanted among the untidiness.

Old cups and saucers were scattered around the floor. A packet of biscuits had rolled under the scruffy settee. A pile of American paperbacks on a table had fallen over, the books scattering across a couple of crumpled newspapers. I would have liked to have stopped and read the papers, but I had no time; as it was I grudged every moment that I spent looking for the shoes, necessary though they were.

I found one at last, behind the colour television set. The other one was at the far side of the room, a pair of brown sneakers which were too big for me and flapped and chafed uncomfortably around my feet as I walked. Even so, they were better than nothing. I was lucky to have shoes at all, and now, at least, I could get away from here, though without money and proper clothes there was no telling where I would get to next.

The thought of looking for my own

clothes crossed my mind, but without anything to work on it would have taken too much time. I pulled open one or two drawers in the sideboard, found a couple of pound notes and some small change, which I slipped into the pocket of my jeans, then I turned to leave.

Anything was better than staying here, especially with the doctor, Kyme, coming back tomorrow to try and make me talk. My flesh crawled at the thought of that, and I went quickly back into the passage, and stood, listening. There was no sound from upstairs and I went quickly along the passage, heading in what I reckoned was the direction of the front door.

I was right. I was as glad to see that door as a starving man would have been to find a free dinner, and I snapped back the catch, stepping into the chill night air.

Now, my problems really began. After the warmth of the house, I was cold, and my eyes weren't yet adjusted to the darkness. In addition, the fight with Sally and Nobby had left me feeling weak and dazed, and what I would really have liked to have done then would have been to lie down and go to sleep. Instead I had to find out where I was, then try and get to somewhere that I was recognized.

Behind me was the bulk of the house, one lighted window showing the living room where I'd found the shoes, another one, right up near the roof, marking the room where I'd been held prisoner, and where Nobby and Sally still were.

I set off down the overgrown drive, not knowing how I was going to overcome my problems, not even sure whether or not they had a sensible solution. I was absorbed in that, trying to find a way out, and I wasn't really looking where I was going.

It was the noise which stopped me in my tracks and made sweat start out on my forehead.

The shrill giggling of Doctor Kyme.

★　★　★

Standing where I was, I could see hardly anything. The darkness combined with the trees flanking the drive to block my view, but even so I reckoned that had the doctor been coming up the drive I should have been able to see something of him. That puzzled me. If I couldn't see him it must mean that he was sneaking about the trees, and if he was such a big pal of Nobby's why should he need to do that? Why couldn't he simply come up the drive? I frowned at the thought, then moved back slowly, towards the house. While he was still hidden in the darkness I wanted to make sure that there was no chance of his sneaking up behind me. Once I had the solid feel of the bricks behind me I felt a whole lot safer and I could give all my attention to the problem.

There was only one answer to it.

He didn't want Nobby to know that he was here.

And there could be only one reason for that. Me. He was as interested in this supposed forty thousand pounds as Nobby, but he didn't fancy the idea of sharing it. That made sense, knowing the type of people they were, and only left two unanswered questions. What was he proposing to do about it, and why was he giggling?

I thought I knew the answer to that one, too.

He must have seen me.

That was a jolly thought to have in the darkness, and when I shivered it wasn't entirely due to the chill night air or the fact that I had no socks on. The only good point I could think of was that Kyme was nowhere near as big as Nobby, but even that didn't do very much to help me. If I was held up for too long dealing with him I had the feeling that Nobby was going to get out of that room. And once he was amongst us again I wasn't going to have the slightest chance.

So I had to get out.

I moved slowly along the front of the building. I still couldn't see anything, other than the trees, which were swaying gently in the darkness, the faint rustling of their leaves covering any slight noises which I might make.

Or Kyme, of course. Not only could I not see him, but I was likely not to hear him either. My ears strained so much that they were in danger of growing points. When I moved, my legs were stiff with tension, and even when I tried to relax I was still on edge.

And then I spotted something. It was only a faint shadow, something slightly darker than the night around, but it was enough. I could tell without seeing any more that it was Kyme, heading towards me, moving just as slowly and furtively as I was myself. If I'd needed proof of what I'd suspected, that would have provided it; he wasn't moving like someone on legitimate business, and in any case I'd heard Nobby say that he'd see him tomorrow, so he mustn't have been expecting him back tonight.

I backed away, retracing my foosteps.

The giggling came again. In the silence which followed I could almost hear the sound of Kyme's breathing.

'Grant,' he said softly. 'Stay right where you are.'

I carried on moving.

'Don't think that I'm guessing,' the doc said, still in the soft, clear voice. 'I know exactly where you are. You can either stop or I shoot.'

I stopped then. Arguing with a gunman when I can't see clearly where he is isn't something that I enjoy doing. I waited right where I was, expecting the crash of a shot at any second. It didn't come, and when Kyme actually loomed up beside me I was so startled that I jumped.

'Not expecting me, were you?' he said, and there was a brittle hardness to his voice which told of strained nerves and tension. 'Now that you're here you've saved me a job.'

My throat was so dry that I could barely speak.

'Have I?'

He nodded. He was still wearing the bowler hat, and with him in that and me in the too-small clothes and big shoes we must have made a worse couple than him and Nobby.

'You've saved me a lot of trouble with Nobby,' he declared. 'He wouldn't have let you go without a struggle. Nobby thinks a lot of you, Grant.'

'Of me or the forty thousand pounds?'

Kyme gave a faint smile. It didn't improve his looks any.

'So you admit to knowing about that?'

'I know what I've been told,' I said. 'I can't remember a thing about it.'

'I'll make you remember,' he said, in the same brittle tone, then he moved the gun slightly. 'Come on. There's no sense in hanging about here in the cold.'

'What if I don't come?'

He shrugged.

'Then I'd have to shoot you.'

'Carry on with it,' I said, with more confidence than I felt. 'Then see how you go on about finding the forty thousand.'

He hadn't thought of that, I could see. While he was working out what to do about it I took a chance that he wouldn't shoot. Jumping forward, I grabbed for his gun hand. The gun went off with a flat crack and I heard the bullet chip against the wall. Then I had him. He fell over backwards as we collided and the gun went off again. This time it was followed by a smashing of glass, but that came too long afterwards for the bullet to have done it.

Seconds later my worst fears were confirmed.

'That you, doc?' Nobby cried.

'I'm trying to stop Grant from getting away!' The doc's voice was high and shrill. I kicked out. My foot caught him under the chin as he lay on the ground, and he made a high, keening sound, like one of those dog whistles which humans can barely hear.

'He's trying to double cross you, Nobby!' I cried, just to help things along, then, freed from the doc's fumbling grip and the fear of being shot I turned and ran.

I wasn't sure where I was going. All that concerned me was to put the house behind me, to get somewhere, anywhere, where I could sit down and think things out without the fear of Nobby walking in at any time. I didn't know what I was going to do after that, for I had no idea what was going on, or even whether there really was forty thousand pounds.

If there was, whose was it? How had I got hold of it? Had anyone helped me? Maybe even Nobby and Kyme had worked with me, which could be why they were in such a flap now. Yet in that case, wouldn't they already know where the stuff was hidden?

And had I really killed a man?

That was the one thing which I couldn't follow. I sensed that if I'd done anything like that it would have left at least some trace in my mind, whatever else had gone. But if it wasn't true why had Nobby brought it up? What could he hope to gain by it? None of it made sense, nor did there seem any way of getting an explanation.

At last I reached the end of the drive and hurried out through rusty wrought-iron gates onto the road. I didn't really know what time it was, but the road was so deserted that I guessed it must be fairly late. I hesitated for a moment, then, as it didn't really matter which way I went I turned left and started to walk. After a few minutes a car sped past. It was followed almost at once by another, and I resolved that when the next one came I was going to try and get a lift. Even though I looked such a ragbag I could always spin some sort of yarn.

In the next fifteen minutes or so I tried several cars. None of them stopped and I was losing hope when I heard the roar of a lorry behind me. The headlamps flashed on full beam, throwing the distorted shadows of myself and the hedgerows onto the road, then I heard the hiss of air brakes.

'Going somewhere, pal?' a voice called above the clatter of the engine.

'The next town,' I said, hoping that he wouldn't think it odd that I didn't know it's name.

'You'd better come up here. Take all night and all tomorrow to walk there.'

I scrambled into the high cab and settled myself into the seat. The engine wasn't as noisy once I'd closed the door, and though conversation wasn't as easy as it would have been in a car it wasn't all that difficult.

I could tell that the driver, although he seemed to be concentrating on the road, was weighing up my appearance, and I tried to hide the pinkness of my ankles poking out of the jeans.

'What made you try and walk?' he asked after a while.

I shrugged.

'I've got no choice,' I said, trying to put on the right kind of voice. 'I was doing a bit of hiking, a few days away from everything, camping out, you know the sort of thing.'

He nodded, and I gave what I hoped was a rueful grin.

'The only trouble is that I set fire to my tent,' I said. 'I knocked over the stove and the whole thing went up.'

He gave me a sideways glance, changing gear for a bend, flashing his headlights as we came into it, lighting up the road ahead as though it had been daylight.

'That was tough luck,' he said. 'I thought those things were supposed to be made so that couldn't happen, even if you did knock them over.'

'They are nowadays, but mine's an old model,' I said, trying to hide the fact that I knew nothing about camping. 'I saved what I could but most of my gear went up with it. My maps, too. That's why I'm not so clear about where I am.'

'You're not so far now from a place called Colley,' he said. 'It's only a little village, but once you get there you can get a bus to Staines, and you'll soon get from there back to London.' He paused. 'I take it you're from London?'

I nodded, though I wasn't even certain about that.

'Got any money?' he asked.

'A little,' I said. 'For once, I wasn't too bothered about my money. I was more interested in saving myself. I can always get more money.'

'That's right enough,' the driver agreed. 'My name's Bob, by the way.'

I told him mine was Ken. For some reason I didn't want to give too much away until I had some idea what was going on.

'Those paraffin stoves pack quite a punch when they go wrong,' I went on, the subject seeming to exert a fascination for me as I sought to elaborate on my story. 'I wouldn't have thought that one could have done so much damage.'

We talked about this for a while, the

driver curious about what had happened, myself trying to think up as many details as I could. I hadn't even seen a paraffin stove for years, let alone done any camping, but he didn't seem at all suspicious. Eventually, after we'd groaned up a steep hill, I saw the lights of an all-night transport cafe ahead.

'We'll have some tea,' Bob said, pulling into the park, which was nothing more than a rutted field. 'They do a good bacon sandwich here, too.'

I held on as the lorry lurched over the uneven ground, Tea and a bacon sandwich suited me fine, and Bob grinned when I said so.

'I'll bet they do,' he said. 'After what you've been through I reckon you're ready for something.'

He was more right than he could ever have known, and I smiled in the darkness as I jumped down from the cab and followed him into the cafe.

It was the usual sort of transport place. Tables, chairs, a pool of cold tea and a half eaten meat pie on one of the tables, nothing fancy. At one end of the room was the counter. At the other, dominating everything, like a sentinel watching to make sure there was no trouble, was a juke-box. Bright, garish, the sight of all those records stacked in the selector struck an odd chord in my mind. I shook my head, trying to clear it, though I knew from past experience that was useless. Apart from ourselves there were only two other people in the cafe, and one of them was the surly looking bloke behind the counter.

He stared at me, then his glum face broke into a smile at the sight of Bob.

'Back on this run again?' he said as we came up.

Bob nodded.

'First trip of the season,' He gestured to me. 'This is Ken. I picked him up on the road after he'd set himself on fire.' He told the story, obviously tickled by it, and then we were served with our food.

We carried it to a table near the silent juke-box, and I stared at it again, wishing that I could remember what it was about it that was so familiar. Had I had something to do with juke-boxes before I came involved with Nobby? That could have been it, but somehow I felt sure that there was more to it than that.

Instead of separate chairs in this part of the cafe there was a long, upholstered bench, serving three tables. Bob was already biting into his sandwich as I put my plate on the table. When I came to sit down I spotted what looked to be an old newspaper crumpled into the back of my part of the bench, and, thinking that there might be something in it which would tell me what was going on, I picked it up.

'I've been out of touch with the news for a day or two,' I said to Bob as I opened it.

He looked at me curiously.

'That's been lying around for months,' he said, 'and it isn't even a newspaper. It's — '

But I wasn't listening to him. I'd opened the paper and found a photograph on one of the inside pages. The photograph was of me but the name underneath it wasn't mine, and as I stared at it everything tumbled back into place. Looking at the truck driver I could see that he knew too, and I was suddenly more afraid than I'd been for years.

2

If I hadn't thought I could sing I should never have met Stan White, and I shouldn't have been in the jam which I've just been telling you about.

And if I hadn't been stupid enough to go to a holiday camp with some friends of mine, about five years prior to my getting in the jam, I would never have thought that I could sing.

Actually I'd never been keen on the whole holiday camp idea. I'm not really the mixing, party-giving type who thrives in the sort of atmosphere in which those places specialize, but the mates with whom I was going around at the time thought it would be a good idea, with everything planned, plenty of birds and no need to look for them, that sort of thing, and rather than holiday on my own I reluctantly agreed to go along with them.

The first day, during which we were left

pretty much to ourselves, wasn't so bad, but on the second I ran into one of those sexy birds specially employed to whip up the right atmosphere and draw mugs like me into the fun and games. At first I wasn't having any, but it soon became clear to me that when she collected her weekly pay envelope the owners of the camp weren't wasting their money. She took me for an on-the-house drink, and with a few flutters of her long, false eye-lashes and hardly any help at all from an ultra-short skirt and tight sweater she talked me into entering a talent competition which was held that night.

To this day I don't know why I eventually agreed. After she'd gone I remember thinking for an hour or so that it might not be such a bad idea after all, and then realizing just what I'd let myself in for. As soon as I made my decision I hurried to find her; she must have been used to things like that, and with smiling charm she brushed aside everything that I said.

'Nonsense, Matt,' she said. 'I'm sure you'll be fine once you get up there.'

'But — '

'I know there's a twenty-five pound prize for the winner, but it's still only a bit of fun,' she went on firmly. 'No one expects very much.'

Maybe they didn't, but I still wasn't convinced. My mates thought the whole thing was a gas, and that evening found me on the stage, in front of what seemed more like half the town than a few holiday makers at one camp.

I won it.

All I did was get up there and sing for five minutes. In return I got twenty-five quid, plus the pick of the birds for the rest of the fortnight that I was there.

I was Matt Grant. Being seen with me was the in-thing for the younger females, and as far as I was concerned I didn't mind a bit. Not only that, but I'd enjoyed my brief few minutes in front of the spotlight far more than I ever thought I would, and I was sorry when the fortnight came to an end.

Had I known it then, things were only just starting.

Waiting for me when I got back to my

flat was a letter from a guy called Marvin Freeman. In it, he offered his services as my agent. According to him, one of his scouts who had been at the contest thought that I had promise beyond a mere holiday camp and had recommended me. I reckoned that the letter was a big send-up, but as he was paying all the expenses I'd nothing to lose by going along to see him.

He wasn't at all the kind of person I'd expected. Instead of being big and fast-talking and pseudo-American, he was little and thin and talked fairly slowly, with an accent that was an odd mixture of Devon and Yorkshire.

'Right, lad,' he said, after his secretary had shown me into his office, a pretty small place in an old block in Soho, but well furnished for all that. 'Sit down.'

I sat down in an armchair drawn up in front of the desk and looked round, waiting for him to speak. He held his hands a few inches above the desk, his fingertips reflected in its polished top, then he lowered them slowly.

'You've seen my letter, lad,' he said.

'What do you think of it?'

'Not much,' I said in an off-hand tone.

'Now look, lad — '

'And my name isn't lad,' I told him. 'It's Grant. Mr Grant to you.'

His thin body stiffened. His face glowed red, like one of the turnip lanterns we used to make as kids, and his mouth worked, opening and closing without a sound. I reckoned that I was getting him where I wanted him now, and before he could make any answer I went on:

'This scout of yours. If he was at the contest what was wrong with him approaching me there and then? Surely he could have made whatever offer you're going to make?'

Freeman gave me an easy smile. He had the air of someone answering a question which had been asked over and over again in the past.

'That's not the way we work, lad, Mr Grant,' he said. 'My scouts don't have the power to negotiate terms or make offers. All they do is recommend people to me. Apart from that, immediately after that contest you'd have agreed to anything that had been suggested to you. We like to wait a week or so, give you a chance to cool down, so that there's no implication that we're trying to put one over on you.'

'All right,' I said, settling back in my chair. 'I'm here now so I might as well listen to the rest of what you've got to say. I don't have to agree to anything if I don't like it.'

'Not a thing, if you don't want to,' he agreed, 'but when you know what I've got to offer I'm quite certain that you'll change your mind. I wouldn't have dragged you here if I hadn't thought it would be worth your while.'

He talked on. I didn't realize it at the time but the persuasion techniques were much the same as those that the girl at the camp had used, the same as any advertiser or promotor would employ, a golden web of talk, stressing the advantages, mentioning the disadvantages so that no one could say he'd left them out, but skating lightly over them, as if they didn't count so much. By the time he'd finished telling me what sort of money I could earn as a pop singer I was half convinced, and I imagine that he could tell that I was from the expression on my face.

'Think it over, Mr Grant,' he said, leaning back and offering me a cigar, which I declined. He took one himself, lit it and got it going nicely. 'Rush decisions are no use to me. You might change your mind again in a week or two. The contract would bind you legally, but that isn't the way I like to work. I'd rather things were nice and friendly than done to the letter of the law.'

'Suppose things don't work out,' I asked him, watching the reflection of the glowing cigar tip in the top of the desk, so that he wouldn't be able to tell from my eyes how near I was to being persuaded. 'Where would I be then?'

'Back where you started,' he said with a grin. 'A clerk in a crummy office. You wouldn't have lost anything but if you don't take this chance now you'll never get another. Why spend the rest of your life wondering what you might have missed?'

He didn't know it, but that was more or

less the clincher. If I didn't sign on with him I'd never know what might have happened, and after another five years or so of pushing a pen in an office I'd probably feel like throwing myself under a truck.

Freeman went on urging me, not obtrusively, but answering some of the questions which he knew would be bound to come into my mind sooner or later. Even if I didn't become a big star, he said, there was plenty of gravy at the bottom, more than there was in any office. And there wasn't only money. As a pop singer, people would be interested in what I did. I'd be able to have pretty near any bird that I fancied.

'And don't forget,' he said, 'that for all this you'll only be working two or three hours a night. Plenty of time for the birds.'

I tried to look as doubtful as I could, hoping that he might increase his offer.

He didn't. More than anything else, that convinced me that he was on the level.

'Think about it, lad,' he urged, slipping

back into his old manner. 'Let me know in a day or two what you've decided to do.'

I thought about it. I also made a few enquiries and found out that Marvin Freeman was a genuine agent, though he had no big names amongst his clients. Maybe that's what he was after, and had me lined up for the spot. Either way, I didn't see why he should waste his time with me if he didn't genuinely think that I could make money for him; and if I made it for him, I'd make it for myself as well.

'You've done the right thing, Matt,' he said, when I told him. 'Give me a couple of months and you'll be a big name. Just wait and see.'

It took longer than that. To start with he wouldn't let me sing at all for a month, insisting that I spend the time with a friend of his named Isaacs who would teach me all he knew about stagecraft and presentation. That was a boring grind, and I think that by the end of it Freeman sensed that I was getting restless.

'We'll soon have you out on the road, lad,' he said when I called in to pick up the weekly money which he was paying me. 'I've got you a couple of bookings for next week.'

'How do I go on for musicians?' I asked.

'Don't worry about a thing,' he said. 'I've got a nice little group together for you.'

'Who pays them?'

'You do, pal,' he said, the surprise in his voice showing that it hadn't occurred to him that there might be any other way. 'You'll get a fat fee for anything you do, and out of it you'll have to give the lads their weekly salary and pay my commission. There might be the odd bill for promotional stuff, too, from Isaacs.'

'You take your percentage from the gross, I suppose?'

'I've got to, lad. I get a percentage of your earnings, and the fee is what you earn. What you do with it after is your own concern.'

It might sound strange, but up until then I hadn't looked at it that way. However big the fee was, I wouldn't have much left after everyone had had their cut, including the taxman. Cynically, I wondered how much Isaacs paid Freeman for the business he was getting, but I didn't ask about it; it wasn't really anything to do with me.

I needn't have worried. We were billed as Mr Mawson's Magic Vine, a name suggested by Isaacs, and right from the start we went down well. Freeman was good at getting us bookings, and fees spiralled so much that I had no trouble in paying all the bills and keeping a good slice for myself. I cut myself off from my old, dead-end life, and that was where my troubles started; the people I was in with now were a fast, showbiz set, more established than I was, a lot of them with safe investment income as well as their earnings. To keep up with them I had to spend pretty freely, run a big car and wear flash clothes. When the ready money ran out, I had the bills sent to Freeman, and though he paid them easily enough I found that the money was taken out of my fee; that didn't matter so much at first, but then I realized one week that I hadn't enough in hand to pay the lads, let alone provide for myself.

After a few minutes' thought I went to see Freeman.

'Come in, Matt,' he said, shuffling some papers to one side and taking the inevitable cigar out of the box. 'Have a seat. I've got something to tell you.'

'And I've got something to tell you,' I said. 'I've run out of money.'

'What do you mean?'

'Tomorrow, the lads are going to want their wages. I've not enough in the bank to pay them.'

'What about all that you got from the Lazy Daisy for that week?'

'It's gone on other running expenses,' I said, not wanting to tell him that most of it had been spent on birds and booze. 'I've an image to keep up.'

'You're keeping up an image all right,' he said grimly, 'but it isn't the right one. Now listen, Matt, things have got to change. People don't want the kind of pop star that you're trying to be any longer. They want someone who's more sensible, someone they can respect.'

I thought he was wrong, but it was

better not to argue too much.

'I don't seem to be doing so badly,' I said, in token defence of what I was doing.

'You're not. And you'll do even better in the future.' He picked up some sheets of foolscap which were lying, stapled together, on the desk. 'Know what this is, lad?'

'I haven't got a clue,' I told him, thinking that it was just another club engagement. 'I leave all that to you. That's where a lot of my money goes, paying you.'

'And value you get for it too. This is a recording contract, lad. It'll really put you and the Magic Vine on the map.'

A recording contract. That was something we'd dreamed about, something which we thought would really put us in the money.

'Shouldn't we have gone to an audition?' I asked, suddenly wary.

Freeman shook his head, then stuck his cigar in the corner of his mouth, where it wagged up and down as he spoke.

'They don't do things that way

anymore. It makes for too artificial an atmosphere. They use scouts, now, like I did when I found you.' He paused. 'I'll lend you some cash for now. You'd better get the lads together and we'll plan what we're going to do as a record.'

We made several records. The sessions were supervised by a thin, gawky character who argued with us over which one should be released; he won simply because it was his company's money which was at risk, but he mustn't have been as gawky as he looked for the disc went right into the hit parade.

Could be that it was just luck, but the second one we made did the same and suddenly we were a talking point in the musical press. I spent more heavily than ever, but that didn't matter because there was a lot coming in.

At least, I thought it didn't matter.

'You're going through this money too fast, Matt,' Freeman told me one day with a worried frown. 'You'll wake up some morning and find that you haven't a penny.'

I was in a good mood that day.

'Don't bank on it,' I said, and laughed. 'Get it, Marvin? You told me I'd have no money and I said — '

'You said not to bank on it.' Freeman's voice was gloomy; with him, you didn't joke about money. 'I'm warning you, Matt.'

'I heard you. How are the orders for *Rim Ram* going?'

'Much the same as the last two.' He paused. 'These are only advance orders, Matt. The shops have still to get rid of them.'

'They'll manage,' I said. *Rim Ram* was our latest single, and I thought very highly of it, though some people said it was nowhere near as good as the others. 'You see, Marvin. In another week or two we'll have more money than we've ever had.'

We didn't. For some reason *Rim Ram* didn't take off. I kidded myself that it was some fluke of the market, but eventually I had to agree with what everyone else was saying. It just wasn't any good, and it was obvious even to me that with the last two records the public had bought them for the song rather than the fact that it was me singing it. Unless we could find a song as good as the others we were going to be sunk.

So I thought that was going to be easy. It wasn't.

After a frantic fortnight of grubbing around, during which the expenses of keeping the act together continued unabated, I realized that it wasn't going to be so easy. Worse, although we had quite a few bookings for personal appearances, they would soon fall off when our name dropped off the public's lips.

'You'll have to do something,' I said to Freeman. 'You're my agent.'

'I can't write songs, Matt. Neither can I make the teenyboppers buy your records if they aren't any good.'

'What do you mean, no good?'

'The last one wasn't. Neither was the one before that, if you ask me, but it sold. That's one point in its favour.'

'It's a damned big one,' I growled. 'How about bookings?'

'They're still all right,' Freeman said. 'I

don't know how long that'll last, but there's a month's work guaranteed.'

I would have thought that we'd have been able to find a suitable song in four weeks, but we couldn't. Freeman didn't seem too bothered by it; he simply suggested that they weren't writing my type of song and that if I waited a while one would come along.

'That's no good to me,' I said. 'I've the boys to keep together. Isn't there some way you can get a record in the charts without people actually buying it?'

'There are one or two ways,' Freeman said after a pause. 'You can either go round to the shops which supply the figures for the charts and buy up enough copies to ensure that they return it. Or you can have a word with the right people and see if they'll help you. Hyping, it's called.'

I knew what it was called and I felt like telling him so. The theory is that once a record is seen to be in the charts people who want to stay trendy will buy it of their own accord, and it will soon start to sell.

'Well?' I said to Freeman. 'What are you waiting for? Get on with it. By this time next week we should see *Rim Ram* making an entry.'

Freeman looked unhappy. His cigar was on the edge of the desk, with about half an inch of ash on it. He ignored it and looked at me instead.

'Hyping costs money, Matt.'

'Well? I've got money, haven't I?'

He didn't answer the question directly. 'There was a letter from your accountants this morning. They've settled last year's income tax and they want a cheque from you to clear it.'

If there was one thing that could make me forget *Rim Ram* for the moment it was income tax.

'How much do they want?'

'Four thousand nine hundred.'

'Couldn't they have made it a round five thousand?' I asked with a grimace. 'I suppose there's no way out of it, is there?'

He shook his head.

'You don't seem to get the point, Matt. You've only got two hundred and thirty in the bank.'

Two hundred and thirty. It sounds a good bit, but with normal running expenses coming out at somewhere near two hundred a week, and a tax bill of nearly five thousand, it was nothing at all. He couldn't have given me a greater shock if he'd hit me.

'How have things got like that?' I asked him, leaning over the desk in sudden anger.

'You've spent it, lad, not me.'

'But you were supposed to watch it and tell me when things were getting low.'

'I've been warning you for weeks, Matt,' he said wearily. 'I've told you until I'm sick of it that you were overspending. What are you going to do about this tax?'

'When do they want it?'

'Right away.'

I leaned so far over the desk that when his mouth opened in a little cry of astonishment I could see the fillings in his teeth.

'They can't bloody well have it, can they?' I said. 'If you want them to have it you'd better get me some bookings.'

He laughed softly.

'I can't get you bookings at the price you're used to,' he said. 'You're washed up, Matt. Now that you aren't in the charts people don't want to know. At the only fee I could get for you now it would take you a year to pay just that tax.'

'What do you mean, I'm washed up? Just because one record hasn't — '

'Things move fast in the pop world,' he said blandly. 'If you want to keep things moving you've got to hustle. That's the way of it, Matt.'

I stood up and looked at him. He was smiling blandly, but when I thought of it afterwards he could afford to smile. With the caution born of experience he'd taken his cut first, and he was probably the only one of my hangers-on to whom I didn't owe money.

'That's the way of it, is it?' I said, forcing the words out. 'Is that all you've got to say?'

'Not much else I can say, is there?'

I stood back looking at him. Suddenly I smiled, and I saw a puzzled frown start to creep over his face, his expression changing as he wondered whatever I could have to smile about, in my position. He soon found out. I drew back my hand and slapped him across the face, once twice, three times. The slaps sounded like pistol shots. His head rocked from side to side. He made no attempt to defend himself.

After I'd hit him a few times I felt better. I gave him one last crack, hitting him so hard that he went over sideways, and the echoes of the slap mingled with the sound of the falling chair and his feet thudding against the underside of the desk. Without looking at him I turned and walked out of his office. Any problems that I had from now on I would have to solve by myself; the first one seemed to be to get myself a new agent, but that wasn't as easy as it sounded.

All of them wanted to know why I was leaving Marvin Freeman. It was well known that he'd discovered me, and it wasn't hard for them to guess that there must be something radically wrong if we were splitting up. Whether or not anyone spoke to Freeman in the day or so that I was going the rounds I don't know, but certainly no one wanted me as a client. When I tried to get new bookings on my own the situation was even worse; I hadn't the first idea how to go about it, and all the promotors I contacted wanted to know what had happened to my agent. It was the same old vicious circle, and there didn't seem any way of getting out of it.

On top of that was the tax bill and the wages for the group at the end of the week. By selling my car I could meet the wages for a week or so and keep the lads together, but after that there was nothing, If I didn't think of something soon I was going to drop back to the dead end from which I'd come, but my mind was a blank. I could think of nothing.

All I could do was sell my car to stave off the break-up for another week, ring the accountants and promise them a cheque as soon as I'd sorted out my temporary difficulties, as I phrased it, and move to a cheaper flat. Nothing that I did was any good, and soon, with only ten pounds left in the bank, it was obvious that I was going to have to get a job of some sort.

What a come down! Me, pop singer Mr Mawson, working in a normal job. After casting around for a while to find something with at least a promise of money I ended up as a door-to-door salesman.

It wasn't much, but at least it gave me some money, and as I tramped the streets I could plan the comeback I was sure I would make, some day. It was just a question of waiting for the right breaks, I told myself. Sooner or later it was bound to happen.

Presently, about two months after I'd taken the job, I called at a block of flats with my case of samples. It wasn't the sort of place from which I expected much, but I had an hour or so before the time I usually finished and rather than do nothing I thought I might as well try to make another pound or so.

I did the ground floor and made a few sales, then went up to the next one. There was nothing to tell me that the door halfway along the corridor was any different from the rest of them, but if I'd known what was to happen through my calling at it I'd have left the flats there and then.

But at that time I knew nothing of the future. Raising my arm, I knocked on the door of flat twelve.

★ ★ ★

The door was opened by a young woman. Now, with all this a long time behind me, I can make a blunt statement like that; at the time, seeing her was like picking up a bare wire, not knowing that the current was turned on. It wasn't even as if she was beautiful. She wasn't, in the accepted meaning of the word, though pretty was too pale and weak a way of describing her. She had a presence, a quality, something impossible to define but worth far more to her than anything about her face or figure.

Not that there was anything wrong with that. There wasn't. Added to everything else, it made her sensational.

'Well?' she said, looking at me with the blank stare which people keep for strangers in whom they aren't particularly interested.

I swallowed. My mouth had gone dry, and the sales talk which normally flowed so glibly suddenly seemed stilted and inadequate.

'I've got one or two things here that I'd like to show you,' I began opening my suitcase. 'It won't take more than a few minutes and it could be that there's something which will interest you.'

'I don't think so,' she said, giving me an amused smile and flicking the ends of her blonde hair back over her shoulders. 'But you can try if you want. I'm not doing anything important right now.'

It was hardly the most promising of starts, but now that I'd made an opening I found it easier to go on. I took the articles from the case, one by one, suddenly conscious of how cheap and tawdry most of them were. She didn't say anything, which is one of the most daunting ways to treat a salesman. Arguments you can counter, even insults give you something to work on, but a complete silence leaves you up in the air.

All you can do is go on talking, hoping that your approach is the right one and that sooner or later the prospect will give some indication of whether or not you're getting home.

With this girl there was nothing.

Nothing, that is, except the amused smile, as if she was thinking what an idiot I was.

By now I was almost at the end of my range. It was starting to look as though I'd been wasting my time here, that she'd let me go through everything just for the fun of it. Normally that would have made me good and mad, but this time she was so attractive that I wouldn't have minded; it was enough to have an excuse for talking to her, and a sale as well would merely be so much extra bunce.

I'd given that sales talk so often that once I was launched on it I could do it without thinking. All the time I was speaking I was trying to think of some way in which I could get to see her again; it wasn't easy and her own attitude was far from encouraging.

I reached the bottom of the suitcase. I

always saved the best thing until the last when the pitch looked like going on for a long time, and now I took it out. A big teddy-bear, which I reckoned would be a sure-fire seller nearer to Christmas, if the way it was going now was any guide.

As soon as she saw it I could see that I had her attention. Stepping up the patter I began to concentrate entirely on making the sale.

'Can I have a look at it?' she asked, holding out her hand. Her voice was soft and clear, entirely in keeping with her appearance.

I gave it to her. She held it close to her, almost as if it was a baby, or one of those small dogs that girls like her go for. There was something incredibly suggestive in the way she was fondling it, and I felt the beads of sweat starting out on my forehead.

'It suits you,' I said, baring my teeth in what I hoped was a natural grin.

'Maybe it does,' she said. 'I might be able to use it in my act.'

'Your act?' I got onto that right away. Apart from being something on which I could hook the rest of the sales talk, it was the first contact I'd had with show business in a good few months, and it might have been the break I was waiting for.

'That's right,' she said, still fondling the teddy bear. 'I do a bit of singing and dancing at a few clubs.'

'I used to be on the stage myself,' I told her.

'Really?' she said indifferently, obviously thinking that it was just another angle which I was using. 'How much did you say this bear was?'

I told her the price. She pursed her lips when she heard it and, quick to see that I was in danger of losing the sale after all, I said that I could get one or two more things in the same line, if she wanted to see them.

'You can do that if you want?' she said, 'but I'm not saying that I'll buy any of them. This bear's something like what I'm after, but I think it's too much to pay.'

I knew what I was after but I didn't tell her. We agreed that if I wanted to come back at the same time tomorrow and bring some other samples, she'd look at them, and I left it at that. I was happy enough. There was a chance of a sale, but better than that I was going to see her again. If I could just keep things moving there was no telling what might come of it.

There was no telling what might be waiting for me at home either. I still got the occasional fan letter, forwarded by Marvin Freeman, but I knew as soon as I saw the envelope lying behind the door that it was no fan letter. They don't come in white foolscap envelopes, to start with, and as a rule they don't have typewritten addresses.

Nor are they addressed to me in my real name. Mostly they're addressed to the group or the record company. They send them to Freeman and he sends them to me.

I picked it up, stared at it for a moment or two, and then ripped it open. As I'd guessed, it was from my accountant. The five thousand pounds of tax was still unpaid; not only that, the accountant pointed out, but so was his own bill, of which he had pleasure in enclosing another copy, in case I had mislaid the original.

Mislaid, hell. It had gone to the best place for it, in the waste basket. That still didn't mean I wouldn't have to pay it, but it was easier to forget that way, easier to pretend that there were no bills, and that I was managing to struggle along on my meagre earnings as a salesman, without a care in the world.

The accountant's bill was steep, but it was nothing compared to the tax. There were some official looking documents in the envelope, too; I didn't go through them, but the gist of them was that the taxman was getting a little stroppy about his unpaid bills.

I was going to have to do something about it soon, but what? I obviously couldn't pay it, but arguing with a government department wasn't the same as arguing with anyone else to whom I might owe money. They could be put off, given a few quid on account and so on. The tax people were likely to prosecute me before very long, and that would do me no good at all.

I crumpled the bill and letter, tossed them gently into the air, and then batted them to the far side of the room as they came down. They didn't reach the opposite wall, landing a few feet short of it, rolling slowly along the carpet and then uncrumpling with a soft crackling sound. Like flames. The flames of all my hopes burning away, disappearing without trace.

After tea I phoned Marvin Freeman at home. There was a long wait before he answered; when he did I said:

'Hello, Marvin, this is Matt Grant.'

'Grant?' he said, as if he didn't remember me. 'I don't recall — ' He broke off, and then gave a faint laugh. 'Of course. How are you, Matt? Still selling, are you?'

'If that was my only problem, I'd be happy,' I said.

'What problems can you have?' he said. 'A single man, a job without any worries to it. I know you aren't making as much money as you used to, but — '

'I've got problems,' I said through my

teeth. 'Five thousand of them. That tax bill, remember?'

'I don't remember,' he said after a pause, 'but even if I did, what would you expect me to do about it? It's your money, your tax. There's nothing I can do about it.'

'You should have done something about it long since. You were my agent. It was up to you to stop me from spending all that I earned, to make sure that there was enough put aside to meet this bill when it came.'

He didn't answer right away. In fact, he delayed for so long that I thought he'd just laid the phone down on the table and gone to bed. Just when I was about to shout to him he came back, an edge to his voice.

'There's a limit to how much I was supposed to hold your hand, Matt. I advised you on your act and made sure you got the best terms. What you did with the money was your own affair. I even found you an accountant. If you've got a quarrel with anyone over this, it's him.'

'I can't get onto him.'

'Why not?' He laughed suddenly, and I gripped the receiver tightly. 'Don't tell me you can't pay his bill either, Matt?'

'I don't have to tell you. You know how much money I've got.'

'Maybe I know that. What I don't know is what you expect me to do about it.'

'I think you're partly to blame for the situation that I'm in,' I said firmly. 'By rights you should pay some of this money but I'm not insisting on that. The least you can do is make me an interest free loan.'

He laughed. It was a genuine laugh, rich and warm, a sound made by someone who was really amused at what I'd just said. It rolled out of the telephone at me, making me wish that I had him in the room so that I could get hold of his rotten little neck and beat his head against the wall.

'Listen, Marvin — '

'You listen to me,' he interrupted. 'I don't agree that I'm responsible for this in any way. You had the money and it was up to you what you did with it. Even if it was my fault I'm in no position to lend you that much, but I can find you someone who'll be glad to. It won't be interest-free but I'll get him to shave his rate down as low as he can. How's that?'

It was better than nothing and, although I didn't say so, better than I'd expected from Freeman. I arranged for him to ring me back when he'd fixed it up, and went to bed feeling easier in my mind than I had done for a while.

Somehow I got through the next day. I didn't sell very much, probably because with thoughts of the last call I was going to make, back at that block of flats, made my approach ragged, but for once I didn't care. Before I went there I called back home to collect the other samples, and while I was there the phone rang.

One of the disadvantages of being in the financial position that I was in is that you're frightened of the phone, in case it's someone asking for money. I was tempted to leave it, but it went on and on and as I was leaving I scooped up the receiver.

It was Freeman's man, offering me a loan. The terms were steeper than I would have liked but I couldn't argue, and at least I could pay him back at so much a week. I agreed, and he said that he'd have all the papers round to me as soon as he could.

Slamming the phone down I hurried out. The loan might be important, but to my mind the call on this girl was more interesting. It seemed much further to her flat than it had done yesterday, and when I finally got there she didn't seem to know at first who I was.

'You said I could call back — '

'Did I?' She frowned. 'Yes, I remember now. I never really thought you would.'

'You mean that you don't want to buy anything after all?' She was looking even better than ever today in a pale blue woollen dress which clung to her so tightly that there wasn't room for much underneath. 'If you've brought me back here just for a joke — '

She laughed. It seemed like everyone was laughing at me recently. First Freeman, and now this girl.

'No,' she said. 'I'll have that bear you showed me when you called before. I always intended to have it.'

'Couldn't you have said that before?'

She shrugged.

'I like to make people work for their money. If you'll wait a minute I'll get it for you.'

She turned away from the door and went into the flat. While she was gone I stepped into the hall, leaving my suitcase on the mat. She raised her eyebrows when she came back and saw where I was.

'I don't recall asking you in.'

'You didn't. It's just that it's more comfortable here than outside.'

'More comfortable?' Her voice took on an odd note, not quite fear but not far from it. 'Comfortable for what?'

'Don't worry, lady,' I said. 'I'm not going to hurt you. It's just that having sold you the bear I'd like to see it used. If I could come and watch your act some night.'

She rustled the pound notes she was carrying to pay me.

'You don't have to ask me for that,' she said. 'Anyone can come. That's what the club's there for.'

'Which club?' I asked patiently, a little

brought down because it didn't seem to matter to her whether I came or not.

'I work at half a dozen. When would you be coming?'

'Tomorrow or the night after.'

She gave me the names of a couple of places, and then unexpectedly she smiled.

'If you think I'm any good come round the back and tell me,' she said. 'Get hold of one of the waiters and tell him you want to see Lindsay Ogden. That'll tell him you're a friend of mine because not everyone knows my real name.'

I had the impression that I was really getting somewhere with her then, and not even the thug who came to see me later that evening could alter my good mood.

Thug is the only way of describing him. At first I thought he must have the wrong address, but it turned out that his name was Canston and he was the man with whom Freeman had arranged the loan. A big man, with one of those ugly faces that women either love or hate. Me, I hated it on sight, and I didn't think it was helped by the thin moustache or the way his nose was flattened, as if his face had been pressed into the ground by a powerful piston.

One thing he could do was talk. As someone who was trying to be a salesman I envied him the way the words poured out of his mouth, a stream of reasons why I would do well dealing with him, of reassurance in case I was hesitant about borrowing so much money and of answers to the questions which I might have asked but didn't because I couldn't get a word in. When I signed the papers I was in something of a daze, and I didn't even realize that the thing he was pressing into my hand was a cheque.

For five thousand five hundred.

'Fixed it up specially quickly for you, Mr Grant,' he said, his lop-sided face breaking into a grin. 'Anyone who Mr Freeman recommends is all right with me.' He stood up to go, and the grin faded slowly, as if it had decided that it had no place on a face like his. 'Just one thing, Mr Grant. I'm doing this as a favour to you, because I wouldn't normally lend so much money to someone whose income is as low as yours.

Just make sure that you keep up the repayments and there'll be no trouble.'

'There won't be any trouble,' I said tightly. 'I can promise you that.'

'Then that's fine, Mr Grant,' he said, lowering his voice. 'I get real mean when there's trouble.'

'You'll be all right with me,' I told him, and slammed the door shut.

At the time I really meant that, of course, but things didn't work out quite the way I'd planned. First, I sent the cheque off; once the tax people were off my back I felt a whole lot better, and had I concentrated on the job then I might have managed to pull through.

I didn't.

For one thing, I went to see Lindsay's act a couple of nights later. I was biased, but she was better than even I'd expected. She used that teddy bear in a way that the makers had never intended, too, building a whole erotic fantasy out of it that had the crowd, mainly men, yelling for more. When she finished, I stood up using my handkerchief to wipe the beads of sweat off my forehead.

When I asked a waiter if I could speak to her he looked doubtful at first, but then my use of her real name reassured him and he led me through a yellow door at one side of the club and along a dusty passage. Her dressing room was at the far end, and by the time I reached it she was already out of her stage costume, and wearing her street clothes.

She looked up as I walked in.

'Hi, Matt,' she said, when she saw who I was. 'Think that bear was worth it?'

I started to agree with her, then out of the corner of my eye I spotted that someone else was in the room. A little guy, with hair almost to his shoulders and a small, pointed beard. He was wearing purple trousers and a yellow shirt. Round his neck was a chain made of huge, gold links which matched the motif on his cowboy-heeled shoes. A dazzling figure, really, when you got him in the full glare of the lights, like I did.

'Hi,' I said, uncertainly.

'Yeah, man.' He held up his right hand. It was the sort of hand that would have looked right on a bloke about six feet tall;

on him it was massive and clumsy, as if he'd strapped a couple of shovels to his wrists for a joke.

'This is Matt Grant,' Lindsay said to him. 'He's the one who sold me the bear. Matt, this is Stan White. My boyfriend.'

'Sure,' I said. 'Your boyfriend.'

White grinned at me as I said that, and I had the feeling that he was silently telling me to lay off. To add to the effect he slapped one of his massive hands against the side of his chair, making a sound like a wet fish falling from a table onto the floor.

I tried not to bother, but all the time I was there, and while Lindsay was, if anything, friendlier than before, there was a definite coolness about White.

Not that I blamed him. I wanted his girlfriend, and I didn't care whether he knew it or not.

That was what really led me into deep water. To get her I had to compete with him, and he spent money so fast you'd have thought he'd had a private tip that it would be worthless by tomorrow. I did a little gentle digging, but beyond the fact that he was a dress designer I couldn't come up with much. In trying to cut down his lead I soon ran through my own money, and started to borrow off the firm that employed me. We were allowed to have advances against commission up to a certain extent, and I was soon into them for as much as I could get.

Then, because I was spending too much time thinking about Lindsay, brooding on how I could get rid of White, the orders began to fall off. Through my borrowing, I was already working on reduced commission, and with the greatly reduced salary I could barely afford to live and meet the payments on the five and a half thousand loan which Canston had made me. At first that didn't bother me too much, and with one thing and another I missed a payment.

When it was a week overdue Canston came to see me.

'Guess what I'm after,' he said with a big smile.

Looking at his size and his thin moustache I knew that I couldn't hope to match a smile like that. I did the best

I could, but my face felt stiff and clumsy, almost as if it belonged to someone else.

Right then I wished it did.

'I'll pay you at the end of the week,' I said. 'I'm a bit hard up at the moment.'

His eyebrows raised. He came further into the room and closed the door.

'How about something to be going on with?'

All I had in the world was three pounds, and I needed that to live on for the week.

'I can manage a quid,' I began, but he cut me short with a laugh.

'A quid? That's funny, isn't it?' Suddenly he was very close to me, crowding me so that I could scarcely breathe. 'Suppose I was this bird you're running around with? You'd have more than a quid to spend on her, I'll bet.'

'Look, Canston — '

The words gurgled away as he grabbed my collar. He shifted his grip then plucked me off the ground. As my feet scrabbled at the carpet his fist smashed into my face with a force that knocked me right back against the wall. I tried to stay on my feet but I couldn't manage it; as I slid slowly down the wall his knee came up with perfect timing and caught me under the chin. Through the haze which began to fold itself round me I heard his voice.

'There's one like that for every week that you're overdue, Grant. If the next payment falls behind too, then two of us will come to see you.'

I didn't see or hear him leave, but when I opened my eyes he'd gone. Struggling to my feet I went into the kitchen to make some coffee. With a lot of scrimping I might just about have been able to pay him at the end of the following week, but by then another payment would be due and I'd be no better off.

I shuddered at the thought of two of them coming.

Or even another tangle with Canston.

Not only that, but I wasn't really getting anywhere with Lindsay. I'd taken her out three or four times, but that was all; she still seemed more interested in White, though I couldn't tell whether or not it was for himself or the money that he had.

Maybe he'd lend me some. But then I'd only be in debt to someone else, and somehow owing money to him would be worse than owing it to Canston. I couldn't see any way out, and I felt trapped.

What I really needed at that point was a miracle, and oddly enough I got one, for White himself phoned me the following evening.

'Listen, Matt,' he said, 'I've got something here. If we play it right it's going to make forty thousand pounds for us.'

★   ★   ★

I didn't go round to see White right away, mainly because I had some idea at the back of my mind that it was better not to seem too eager to follow up whatever it was he was going to put to me. Nevertheless, in the intervening couple of days I found it very hard to concentrate on selling the stuff in my suitcase; by the time I did get to his place I was really ready to listen to what he had to say.

Lindsay was there too. If she noticed my air of suppressed excitement she said nothing, but White gave me a sneering glance as I sat down.

We wasted no time.

'All right,' I said to him. 'You've dragged me here when there are a lot of other things I could be doing. Let's hear this wonderful idea of yours.'

He leaned back in his chair, looking at Lindsay, then he pressed the tips of his fingers together, stretched out his legs and turned his head towards me.

'It's a little matter of some drugs,' he said, half closing his eyes as he stared at me.

'If it's drugs I'm not having anything to do with it,' I said bluntly.

'Why not?' I had the impression that he was startled a little. 'What does it matter, man?'

'Why not!' I burst out. 'I've got some scruples, you know.'

He laughed, and Lindsay looked from one to the other of us. I didn't know how much he'd already told her, and right then I wasn't bothered.

'Scruples,' White said. 'You haven't shown much sign of them up to now, have you? If you want people to believe that you ought to hang out a sign. Matt Grant has scruples. It's the only way they'll ever know.'

He laughed again as he finished and as I half rose from my chair to hit him Lindsay put out a restraining arm, catching me, holding me back.

'Don't start any trouble, Matt,' she said. 'Stan's right, in a way. What does it matter?'

This was a side of Lindsay that I hadn't seen before, but I was too involved in the argument to take much notice.

'Stan never told me that the money was going to come from drug pushing,' I insisted. 'If I'd known that I wouldn't even have thought about coming in with you.'

'Who said anything about drug pushing?' White asked.

'You did. You — '

'I said that drugs were involved, but

that's not the whole story. Maybe you should start getting all the facts before you go shooting off your mouth.'

I didn't answer that, but waited for him to go on. When he was certain that I wasn't going to speak he said:

'Ever heard of Lou Calloran?'

'The club owner? Of course I've heard of him. No one who's had anything at all to do with clubs wouldn't have heard of Calloran.'

White nodded slowly.

'That's right,' he said. 'A smart operator, Calloran. Started with one club, which was a run-down dump when he took it over. He built it up, bought others, they're all successful places, aren't they?'

'They seem to be,' I answered cautiously, not at all clear what he was driving at. 'The Spanish Egg's his main place and whenever I've been there it's always been crowded. 'But I don't see — '

'Suppose I told you it was a front,' White said softly.

'A front?'

'Mainly.' He waved a hand in the air. 'There's plenty of dough to be made from them right enough, but Calloran has his fingers in a lot of pies which most people know nothing about. Least of all the cops.' He laughed. 'Drugs are only a small part of his operations.'

'Maybe so, but — '

'Why should you worry where the money comes from, anyway? It's still forty thousand quid, isn't it?'

I looked at him, still trying to sort out everything that he'd said. Calloran was a fairly new figure on the club scene, but he'd soon made a name for himself as a man who knew what the public wanted and who set out to give it to them. Whenever I'd seen him he looked prosperous, but there was no reason to suppose that he had any income other than that from his half-dozen clubs.

What White was telling me came as a surprise, and I wondered with a tiny nagging doubt of suspicion how he'd found out about it all.

He was still watching me, waiting for some comment. Over at the other side of the room Lindsay was also watching me, but it was impossible to tell from her expression just what she thought of this scheme.

'Come on,' White said suddenly, impatiently. 'You must have something to say.'

'I'm thinking about it. It's not the sort of thing you rush into.'

He moved his big hands. He wasn't so brightly dressed tonight as he usually was. Yellow shirt, red tie and black jeans. That alone made him impossible to miss, but the thing that really caught the eye was his red shoes, delicately matching his tie.

Since first meeting him I'd made a few enquiries, to see if there was anything I could use to give me an advantage over him with Lindsay. A lot of people referred to him as a pinhead, which might have been an apt description of his physical appearance, but nothing more; inside that pin head was a smart brain and a mind which usually figured all the angles, one after another, like a computer.

Even so, you needed something other than a smart mind to be a successful dress designer.

Whatever it was, Stan White didn't have it.

I knew something about his business, though he had no idea just how much knowledge I had. In the past he'd worked for one or two clothing firms, argued with the management eventually because he thought their ideas and ways of doing things were too old-fashioned, and finally decided to set up on his own. Things had gone well for him at first; so well, in fact, that one or other of the big firms had been interested in taking him over. They'd paid him three thousand pounds as part of the deal, but before the rest of it could be fixed there had been one of those boardroom coups which afflict all large firms from time to time, and as a result they had pulled out.

That had been a couple of years ago.

Since then White's business had been falling slowly, and three thousand pounds doesn't last a man like him for very long.

You'd only to think of the way he spent money on Lindsay to realize that, and to look around his flat.

It was only a small place, but there was

nothing cheap in the way it was furnished. Everything was modern, of course; there was none of this nonsense about conventional wallpaper or carpets, but that didn't make the things any less expensive.

Three walls were streaked with paint, all colours, though mainly red, yellow and blue, the colours running together like water paints that haven't been given time to dry properly. At first it seemed just a mess of colour, but after you'd looked at it for a while you could distinguish subtle patterns, strange designs that appeared to shift and weave everytime you tried to pin them down. To set this off properly the fourth wall was black, relieved only by an occasional gold thread running downwards.

The floorboards had been polished. Flung down in the middle of the room was a colourful rug, the main design on it a yellow Chinese dragon breathing brilliant red flames from its mouth. Lighting was by hidden lamps, which cast a soft, even glow over everything. There was little furniture, and what there was matched the chairs; they were white, bowl-shaped, clinging and superbly comfortable.

It was the sort of flat which needs a lot of money to set up and keep running, because he couldn't afford to have anything in it which was out of date; to do so would ruin the whole effect. That sort of thing dates rapidly, and costs the sort of money which I was sure White didn't have.

So he'd got this plan which was supposed to bring forty thousand pounds between us.

A shade over thirteen thousand each.

The prospect was very attractive, but I wanted to know a lot more about it before I agreed to go in with him.

'Look,' I said to him now as he lounged in one of the bowl-shaped chairs, his big hands pressed together, 'you say that Calloran has forty thousand quid in his safe. Suppose we start at the beginning and you tell me what a club owner's doing with that much loose cash.'

Lindsay said: 'He's entitled to have that much if he wants. He owns the Spanish

Egg and a lot more besides. He's got more than you'll ever have, the rate you're going.'

Something about the tone of her voice needled me.

'So he owns the Spanish Egg,' I said, 'and a few other clubs in London and some in the provinces. Does he own a cheap stripper like you, too?'

'I'm not — '

'Cut it out,' White said sharply. 'We're not here to argue.'

'Too right we're not,' I agreed. 'We're here to listen to you telling us why Calloran has forty thousand quid in a safe at the Spanish Egg.'

'He gets smarter every day, doesn't he?' White sneered to Lindsay. 'I wonder that he hasn't had the brains to think of this.'

'Get on with it, Stan,' she said, a trace of uneasiness in her voice. 'I don't like all this arguing.'

He looked at her oddly, while I grinned at him. After a moment he shrugged, then he said:

'Outwardly, Calloran's set-up looks straight. He's just a bloke who's built up a chain of clubs. He seems to make more money out of them than most people would but the obvious explanation for that is that he knows what he's doing and he takes his chances as they come up. Like I do.'

He gave me a penetrating stare as he said that, obviously expecting me to say something. I threw him off his stride by keeping quiet, waiting for him to go on.

'That's what things look like on the surface,' he repeated. 'Underneath, they're rotten. Calloran has his fingers in more dirty pies than you'd think possible.'

'Including drugs?'

White dismissed the drugs with a wave of his hand.

'He includes everything. Anything that's profitable He has heavy outgoings, of course, to keep his contacts and get information and pay his suppliers, and because of that he keeps a big cash float in a safe at the Spanish Egg. That way, there's no bank account, no cheques or other bits of paper floating around.'

'Does he keep as much as forty thousand quid?' I asked in disbelief.

White nodded.

'You'd be surprised where the money goes on that kind of operation,' he said. 'He needs a lot of information, for a start, then there's the cops to keep quiet, mouths to stop, all that sort of thing. Forty thousand quid's nothing to a man like Calloran, and anyway no one knows it's there. As far as he can tell there's no danger.'

'If he pays people out of it how come no one knows it's there?' I said briefly. 'And if it comes to that, how do you know?'

'Suspicious, aren't you?' he jeered.

'That doesn't answer the question.'

'It wasn't meant to.'

There was a short silence. I could see Lindsay twisting her fingers together, as if what she really wanted was to have nothing to do with the scheme.

'For a start,' White said, 'most of the people he pays don't know that they're dealing with him. All they get is a packet of money through the post.'

'What about the ones who do know?'

His gaze drifted idly to Lindsay's legs.

They were covered up with a pair of blue slacks so it didn't do him any good and he turned his attention back to me.

'The ones who know that they're dealing with him aren't the type who'd give him away,' he said.

'Granting all that, how come you know?'

White grinned at me as I spoke, and it was an entirely different kind of grin from those which he'd given me earlier, a grin in which humour and triumph and a touch of superiority were blended nicely.

'Lindsay told me,' he said.

'Lindsay did?' I exclaimed, jerking my head round.

'That's right.'

I looked at her, fascinated. So far she was still White's girlfriend, but I hadn't got my share of the forty thousand quid yet. When I had . . .

She was staring at me with bored indifference.

'How come you know about it?' I asked.

'I know because I've seen it,' she said in a dull voice, as if she were saying that she knew it was raining because she'd just been out and got wet.

'How did you come to see it?'

'I learn a lot on my trips round the clubs. I might be just a cheap stripper to you, Matt, but I keep my eyes open and I pick up a lot.'

I flushed. I didn't know what had prompted me to make that jibe but it was hardly the way to get more friendly with her.

'And you're sure about it?'

'I'm certain. I wouldn't have said anything if I hadn't been.'

'How do you know it's forty thousand pounds?'

'Because I overheard Calloran talking to someone else about it. Forty thousand was the figure he mentioned.'

'You're asking a lot of questions, aren't you?' White put in suddenly, his eyes narrowing.

'I've got to ask them, Stan,' I said lightly. 'If I don't, you won't tell me. All you're bothered about is the money. You don't seem to care about the risks.'

'Listen, Matt, if we worry about the

risks there isn't going to be much money for any of us, because we'll all be too scared to do anything about it.'

He had a point there, but it didn't alter the fact that there were risks; if we looked at them sensibly I didn't see why they should hinder us. It was better than White's way, which was to pretend that they didn't exist.

'What about the cops?' I asked.

'Forget about them. Lou Calloran doesn't want the cops in any more than we do. Remember that he's not supposed to have that money, and he'd have a hard time explaining to them where it had come from.'

That was true, but there was still something else.

'What kind of rackets is he involved in?'

'Back to that?' White said. 'You name it, Calloran's there. Protection, narcotics, gaming are the main ones. He licenses some of the small-time operators, too. They pay him a fee and he lets them get on with their petty thieving. If they don't pay he has them beaten up.'

'That's what worries me,' I said.

'Rackets like that need a gang to work them properly, and if Calloran's in with some other big shots he isn't going to simply let you walk off with his money. He's going to do something about it. Frankly, I'm more worried about him than I am about the cops.'

'Forget him, man,' White said impatiently. 'How's he going to know where the money's gone? He's never even heard of us, has he?'

That was true as well, but I still thought that something could go wrong. If it did, I guessed that I'd rather have the cops after me than the sort of cut-throats that Calloran would employ.

'He may not know you,' I said, 'and he certainly doesn't know me, but what about Lindsay? He knows her because she works in his clubs. Isn't there a chance that he'll connect her with it and work back from there to you and me?'

I could see that this idea hadn't come into his mind, and for the first time since he'd put the idea to me he looked undecided. His gaze went from me to Lindsay, who tossed her blonde hair back off her face, still looking as bored as she might have done had she been discussing getting a share of a plateful of shrimps.

'Well?' I said, sharpening my voice to try and jerk her out of it. 'Could he trace it back to you?'

'What about you?' she demanded. 'You were pretty well known at one time, weren't you? Won't someone recognize you?'

I shook my head.

'I've been off the scene for long enough to be forgotten,' I said. 'After all, you didn't know me when I came to your door and sold you that bear, did you?'

That was true and there was no way round it. She still tried to find one.

'How can you be sure that everyone has forgotten you'? There might — '

'This is all getting off the point, Lindsay. When that money's stolen is Calloran going to connect you with it?'

'I don't know,' she said. 'You'd better ask him if you really want to find out.'

'Look, this is no time to start being awkward,' I said. 'I've asked you a question and I want — '

White put up his hand to cut me short, then stood up. He went over to her and got hold of her shoulders, tightening his grip and shaking her violently so that her head jerked backwards and forwards and her hair tumbled around her face like golden corn blowing in a gale.

'Well?' he snarled. 'Could he?'

'I don't know,' she said breathlessly. 'You — '

He shook her again, harder than before.

'You'd better snap out of it,' he said, still shaking her, one of his red shoes merging with the flames coming out of the mouth of the dragon on the carpet, the other one standing out startlingly against the yellow background. 'This is important. Don't you want any of the money when we get it?'

As he said that he flung her back so hard that the front legs of the chair left the floor for a moment and then dropped back with a thud.

'Look, Stan,' I said, 'there's no need — '

'There's every need. What she wants is waking up and this is the way to do it.'

I shrugged. I didn't like the way he was mauling her about but with forty thousand quid at stake there was no point in arguing about it. As yet she was still his girlfriend and if he wanted to shake her like a bad-tempered kid with an old doll it was no business of mine.

'I don't think he could,' she said as White released her. 'I don't know if you've seen the layout at the Spanish Egg, but Calloran's office is at the end of a sort of passage about ten feet long. There's only a thin partition separating him from the passage, and if he's talking loudly you can hear what he's saying.'

'There's no chance that it could all be a joke?' I asked.

'I've checked up,' White said. 'The money's there all right. It's just a question of walking in and taking it.' He must have guessed from the expression on my face what I was going to ask next, for he gave me a jeering grin as he went to sit down. 'Before you say anything, Matt, the people I've checked with are reliable. They won't go back to him, and I can trust what they say.'

'It looks like you've got it all sewn up,' I agreed. 'I suppose you've got some tricky plan as well?'

'That's what we've got to discuss,' he said. 'The facts are these. Calloran keeps the money in a safe at the Spanish Egg. We've got to find that safe, but before we can even look for it we've got to get past the guard.'

'Guard?'

White shrugged.

'If you asked Calloran he'd probably call him a night watchman, but I've seen him. He's about as big as a gorilla and I'm pretty certain he carries a gun.'

'His name's Bannen,' Lindsay put in listlessly. 'Before he went to the Spanish Egg he used to work for Paul Little.'

Now I began to understand why she was a bit lukewarm about the idea. All this appeared to be new stuff to White, and I was afraid that an explanation might go some way towards cooling him off too, but there was no way of getting out of it.

'Paul Little?' he said. 'You mean the mobster?'

'He got fifteen years, six months ago,' I said harshly. 'He'd have got longer, but there were some things which they knew about but couldn't prove.'

The cops had been fairly pleased with themselves when they'd finally pulled in Little. There had been pictures of Superintendent This and Commander That in all the newspapers, smiling, quaffing mugs of beer, generally holding out the glad hand to any crook who'd worked with Little and wanted to give evidence against him. Not that many did, because he wasn't the sort of bloke you grassed on. Not unless you wanted a ventilated head, that is. Or a slit throat.

For two years he'd ruled Soho and the East End, mainly by fear, and even now that he was in police hands no one was going to come forward with any kind of proof that might add a few years onto his prison sentence. Little would still have friends on the outside, and those friends would give any witnesses a good going over as soon as the police found something else to interest them.

But he'd still got fifteen years.

With him out of the way men like Calloran were really starting to flourish again, opening up their own rackets for which there had been no room before, maybe half a dozen different operators filling Little's place. Gradually, one of them would emerge stronger than the others, a new Little would arise and the cops would crack down again.

All that was in the future; by the time it happened Little would be about ready to come out of prison.

'How do you know all this?' White said when I'd finished telling him.

I shrugged.

'The pop business isn't all that clean,' I said. 'Little had his fingers there too. Probably Calloran has by now, but he was only a newcomer before Little was put away.'

'Do you know if Bannen gave evidence against Little?'

'You must be joking,' Lindsay said. 'Not many people wanted to, and he wouldn't have done anyway. He isn't that type.'

'That's what I thought,' I said.

'Maybe we could bribe him,' White began, but I shook my head.

'I know his type from what I saw of Little's sidekicks. He'd take your money and then beat your head in. The fact that he's there at all proves there's money in the club, and if Calloran trusts him he must be hot stuff. If he was the type that would take a bribe he'd never have been left on his own with all that cash.'

'All right then,' he said. 'If you're so smart, you suggest how we get rid of an armed guard who could squash the likes of me with one hand and beat you up with the other.'

'He's one of the risks that you'd have had me think didn't exist,' I said. 'If I hadn't asked all the questions that you were getting upset about a few minutes ago I might never have heard of Bannen until I got in the club. There could be other things for all I know. Whereabouts in the club is the safe?'

'Calloran's office,' he answered at once.

'Sure?'

'There is a safe in Calloran's office,' Lindsay said, 'but I don't think it's the one where he keeps the forty thousand.'

I frowned at her.

'For someone who's only a stripper and doesn't seem to be very interested in this operation you know a hell of a lot of the details,' I said. 'Suppose you tell me how you can be so certain of that?'

'It's obvious.' There was a trace of impatience in her voice. 'If anyone breaks into the club the place to look for a safe is in Calloran's office. That's the last place he's going to keep forty thousand pounds in notes, something that he can't report to the police if anything happens to it. He can't be that much of a fool, Matt, or he'd never have got where he is.'

'You're almost as smart as Grant thinks he is,' White sneered. 'Did you work out all that for yourself?'

'It's obvious, isn't it?'

It was now that she'd said it, but I could see that none of it had occurred to him. He was looking at me with a kind of hopeless expression on his face, an expression which cut through all his bluster, showed me things as they really were, and gave me some clue as to why his business was failing. If this was how he treated every difficulty it was no wonder that things constantly went wrong for him. Even forty thousand pounds couldn't drive him on to produce ideas for getting round the problems, and I knew that if the whole idea wasn't to die there and then I was going to have to do something.

'You've got to be prepared to do a little work if you want that kind of money,' I said, by way of trying to cheer him up.

'So where do you think the safe is?' He turned to Lindsay. 'How about you? Any more bright suggestions?'

'I've no idea,' she said. 'Maybe Bannen knows. You can ask him before he hits you.'

White stood up again, his face pale, his lips drawn into a straight line. Before he could reach Lindsay I grabbed his arm and gave it a jerk. He sprawled back in his chair and turned to stare at me.

'What the hell are you doing?'

'Like you said before, this is no time to argue,' I said. 'If you want to fall out with your girlfriend do it some time else. Right now we've got other things to think about.'

He didn't look too pleased and I gave him a mocking grin.

'If you want to fight with someone,' I said, 'go to the Spanish Egg and fight with Bannen.'

That pleased him even less but there was nothing he could do about it. I knew that he was thinking the same as me. It wasn't going to be any fun tangling with Bannen, and if we didn't even know where the safe was anyway it was going to be even less fun.

'There can't be many places in a club like that where you can hide a safe,' he said. 'For a start it would have to be somewhere the public couldn't get to.'

I nodded.

'Here's something else, Stan. When we've got into the club, got rid of Bannen and found the safe how do you suggest we open it?'

He grinned. He looked really pleased with himself, as if he thought that he had the answer to everything.

'Leave that to me, Matt. I'll deal with it.'

'I hope you know what you're talking about, Stan,' I said, giving him a hard stare. 'I don't want to get in there and go to all that trouble just to have you louse things up.'

'I told you to leave it to me,' he repeated harshly. 'I haven't always been a dress designer, you know.'

'You've never been a safe breaker, have you, Stan?' Lindsay asked softly, her eyes on me.

He shook his head.

'I used to work for Casson's, the safe people. I kept my eyes open and did a bit of out of hours practice with the safes in the showroom. I reckoned that there was no knowing when that sort of thing might come in useful and I was right.'

'If you think you can open it, that's fine,' I said. 'Just so long as you're sure.'

'I can handle it.' He smiled slyly. 'Once you've got rid of Bannen, that is.'

I frowned.

'Division of labour,' he said smoothly. 'I open the safe, you get rid of Bannen.'

141

I gave it a moment's thought.

'I'll work something out,' I said eventually, 'but before I start have you any suggestions?'

I knew he hadn't and I knew it irked him to have to admit it, but I liked seeing him discomforted, especially after the way he'd treated Lindsay.

'There is one other thing,' he said.

'What's that?'

'Don't try and double cross me, Matt. That's all. Just don't try and do anything that you think is cute.'

He stared at me as if he knew exactly what was in my mind.

★   ★   ★

Two nights later we broke into the Spanish Egg.

It was a fairly new place, all glitter and quality. On the surface. Once you looked past that you could see it for what it was, a broken-down old shell of a building which would probably be demolished in the next few years. In the meantime, though, Calloran had done it up pretty cleverly, and the type of person it was designed to attract would never look beyond the surface tinsel anyway.

Since I'd spoken to White a day or two back I'd been wondering what was the best way of getting this money. Bannen was the main trouble; once we'd got past him the rest would be simple. At first I'd thought that it might be better to stay away from the club completely, but the more I thought about it the more I realized that if I was going to produce anything like a proper plan of action I needed to see the place.

After all, there was no risk.

Neither Bannen nor Calloran knew me, and would have no reason to pick me out from the other customers. And there were plenty of them. The Spanish Egg was that sort of place.

'Did you see Bannen last night?' White asked me now, stopping the hired car in the mean little alley which ran at the back of the club.

'I saw him', I answered grimly. 'There can't be many people as big as that.'

White grinned. In the darkness I could

just pick out the faint gleam of his teeth. He killed the engine and switched off the sidelights.

'He'd break you in two if he got the chance,' he said. 'Any smart ideas for dealing with him?'

Quietly, we opened the car doors and got out, White bringing with him a small cloth roll containing tools. We padded over the cobbles, the faint wetness of drizzle on our faces, the pavement shining dully in the light of the single street lamp at the far end of the alley.

'I've got one or two ideas,' I said softly to White. 'Our only chance is to take him by surprise. If we can hit him over the head before he realizes there's anyone in the club we've got him.'

White nodded and stopped before the back door. No one seeing it would have connected it with the flamboyant brightness of the front entrance, but I'd made a point of finding it, and having a good look at it in daylight. Provided there was nothing like an alarm worked by light-beams, or anything clever like that, I thought we could handle it.

I was right.

Whatever shortcomings White might have as a businessman, he had that lock open inside two minutes.

We waited, listening anxiously for any sound in the silence which would indicate that Bannen was waiting for us.

There was nothing.

'He hasn't heard us yet,' I muttered.

'If he has he's doing nothing about it. Any idea where he might be hanging out?'

'I had a look round,' I answered. 'I couldn't see so much but there was a little cubby hole with a desk in it. It's only up the corridor from Calloran's office. It's my guess that's the place Bannen uses.'

We were in the club now, the door pushed to behind us, nothing in front of us but an impenetrable blackness. I felt the touch of White's arm on mine, and I realized from his movements that he was pulling something out of his pocket.

'No torches,' I said sharply.

'I'm not so stupid that I'd switch it on. Not until I know where Bannen is. Which is the way to this cubby hole?'

It was difficult getting our bearings in the darkness but once we'd managed it we could make good progress. An empty nightclub is eerie at the best of times; this one was worse than most because there was no telling when Bannen might come out of the gloom.

'Once we're sure that's where he is,' I muttered, 'we'll have to make some sort of noise to get him out. There's no chance of anyone sneaking up on him in there. That's why I'm so sure it's where we'll find him.'

We moved cautiously along the passage. Apart from the occasional sound which we made there was nothing to show that there was anyone else in the club. A few seconds of it was enough to wear raw places on my nerves and by the time we turned the bend in the passage and saw the faint glimmer of light from the pokey cubby hole I was really on edge.

'There's no sign of him,' White muttered. 'Are you sure that's where he is?'

'I'm sure of nothing,' I said, keeping

my voice down, trying not to let White see how on edge I was. 'It's what I'd do in his place.'

'And we all know how smart you are,' White sneered, but I could tell that his heart wasn't in the jibe.

Motioning him to stay where he was I crept nearer to the cubby hole, then crossed slowly to the other side of the passage, so that I could see further into it. All the time, I was expecting Bannen to appear; the knowledge that if he saw me first he would break me into pieces without making much effort caused the sweat to start out on my brow.

At last I could see right into the cubby hole.

Bannen wasn't there.

Half fearful of some trick I kept on going forward, and when no one appeared I turned and beckoned to White. In the darkness I couldn't see him, but he would be able to pick me out because of the light behind me. So would Bannen, who might well have a gun, and the thought caused me to skip round the edge of the door, where I wouldn't make quite such a good target.

'Well?' White said when he reached me. 'What do we do now?'

I looked round. There was a chair, pushed back from a small desk. A paperback book was open, face down, on the desk, and there was the stub of a freshly smoked cigarette in the ashtray.

'I don't like this,' White said.

'Neither do I.' I cast another glance round then gave a faint smile. 'Bannen seems to have taken care of himself. Shall we try and find the safe?'

'I'd rather find Bannen,' he replied, and I could tell from his voice that he was as nervous as I was.

I shrugged.

'Then let's look for him.' As I turned to the door and took a step forwards White grabbed my arm.

'Are you sure this isn't some trick of yours, something you fixed up last night when you came?'

Irritably I shook him off.

'Keep your voice down or you'll have him here. What sort of trick do you think it might be? If I'd wanted to double-cross you like that do you think I'd have gone to all the trouble of breaking in?'

'Maybe not,' he muttered, but I could tell he wasn't wholly convinced. I didn't bother too much. Bannen would convince him soon enough when we ran across him.

'Let's try Calloran's office,' I suggested. 'That's the most likely place to find everything, safe included.'

White agreed and we went out as quietly as we'd come in. The club was a maze of passages behind the stage, and though the office was only next door to Bannen's cubby hole it was round a corner.

As we turned it we both spotted the crack of light under a door further along the new passage.

'That looks like one of the dressing rooms,' I muttered, keeping my voice so low that it was barely audible, even in the stillness of the empty club.

'Think he could be in there?'

'That depends on whose dressing room it is.' The remark sounded even more feeble when I said it than it had done when I'd thought of it, but the way I was feeling, jokes were hardly the most important things I had to worry about.

'You'd better get him out,' White said.

'Yeah. Just like that.' I ran my tongue over my lips and moved to the door. By pressing my ear to it I hoped to be able to take a guess at what he was doing. Everything was silent. I waited a moment or two and then turned back to White. 'It's too quiet.'

He shrugged.

'What do you want him to do? Sing and shout?'

'I don't like it.'

For some reason I was feeling even more uneasy than ever, but the thought of the forty thousand pounds drove me on. I took a bunch of keys from my pocket, and tossed it onto the floor. The sound was like a pistol shot. Even White jumped.

'That ought to bring him out,' I said, grinning at him mirthlessly.

'I hope you're ready for him.'

We waited. Nothing happened, not even when I dropped the keys for a second time.

'I'm going to open that door,' I said.

White started to say something, sounding as nervous as a first night fan-dancer, but I cut him short and turned the handle. I was tensed, ready for Bannen to jump out, but I needn't have worried.

The state he was in, he wasn't going to jump anywhere in a hurry.

He was sprawled across a narrow table which had been set along one wall, and there was a bright red patch on his forehead, where the blood was leaking from a small red hole.

That wasn't everything. Even worse was the sight of an open safe at the other end of the room. That was where Calloran must have kept his forty thousand pounds, but now it was completely empty.

* * *

The safe had been very well hidden, behind some imitation timber framing on the wall. It was revealed by sliding a section of the moulding to one side. This allowed a false panel in the wall to drop

151

down, so that the door could be opened. To take my mind off the sight of Bannen I was admiring the workmanship, but I was dragged roughly back to what was happening around me when White grabbed my arm.

'You swine!' he hissed, pulling me round to face him.

'What do you mean?'

'This is something you've fixed up! You came in here and shot Bannen. You always meant to doublecross me, I could tell by the way you carried on the other night.'

I said: 'We've already been into this. If I'd wanted to do that there were simpler ways than breaking in here with you. I suppose you'll be saying next that I'm in league with Calloran or something.'

He shook his head.

'Just you, Matt,' he said softly. 'I don't think there's much chance of your tying up with Calloran.' He gave a shrill giggle. 'You aren't his type.'

All the time he was speaking he was moving nearer to me. I tried to keep the same distance between us, and it was only when my back pressed against the wall that I realized how far we'd moved.

A fixed, intent look was coming over his face.

'Or maybe it was you and Lindsay,' he said, and his voice was hardly more than a whisper.

'Suppose we get out of here first and then decide who it might have been,' I suggested. 'Someone knew we were coming here tonight. We could be in line for the cops and — '

'I suppose that's what you'd like to see happen!' he cried. 'The cops will arrest me while you go free!'

'Stan — '

'Then you and Lindsay can enjoy yourselves on the money,' He had stopped moving now and was standing just out of my reach. Something in his eyes warned me that he could be dangerous in this mood, but I didn't realize just how dangerous. Not until he reached casually into his pocket and took out a gun. It was only a small thing, but from the way it caught my gaze and held it, it could have been a huge cannon.

'Stan — ' I said again, but he didn't give me a chance to finish.

'Don't think I haven't noticed the way you carry on with Lindsay,' he said. 'I know a lot more than you think, Grant. You've probably plotted this between you, so that you can get the money and throw the blame onto me.'

I moved slightly. He jerked the gun. The light glinted on the barrel and I stopped moving. With him in that mood it was safer to try and humour him.

'It won't work, Grant,' he said. 'Lindsay hates you. You didn't know that, did you, but it's true. She hates you.'

That was a measure of how far gone he was. One minute I was plotting with her to get all the money for ourselves, and the next she hated me. I didn't try to put him straight. I was more concerned about how I could get the gun before he fired. it.

He moved a fraction nearer, but he was still out of reach. At the far side of the room, Bannen sprawled over the table, the fingers of one hand clenched, almost in the pool of blood which had spilled from his head. Nearer to me the open safe leered down, mocking the three of us, and then I heard White's voice hissing out of the silence.

'I'm going to kill you, Matt. And when I've done that I'm going to kill Lindsay. No one doublecrosses me.'

'No one's trying to.'

He smiled, a slow sad movement of his lips spreading over his face.

'I'll be sorry to see her go,' he said, 'but I've got no choice. I'll have to kill both of you.'

I saw his finger whiten as it squeezed the trigger. The end of the barrel seemed to be a gaping death hole. As I saw his finger move I dropped. The bullet smacked into the wood, right where my head had been. Without giving him chance to realize what I was doing I carried on moving, jumping towards him in a strange, crouching way, my eyes on the gun which was swinging towards me.

Bannen's dead face seemed to grin at me.

It was as if he was saying that he knew what it was like, he'd been through it all himself.

155

As I grabbed White the gun went off again. I felt the bullet tug at my sleeve, then White gave a hoarse cry as he went down beneath me.

'Swine!' he yelled, and his voice echoed round the small room with almost as much noise as the shots.

I smashed my fist into his mouth. The cry cut off at once. His teeth caught sharply on one of my fingers. I smashed down again, putting my full weight on him as he squirmed. The gun was somewhere beneath him, but as long as it wasn't pointing at me I didn't care.

I nearly didn't care about anything. One of his spade-like hands smacked me across the face. By the time my head had finished singing he almost had the gun free and it was only by chopping him down desperately with the edge of my hand that I managed to save myself. Blood was flowing from my fingers where I'd cut them on his teeth. I shook it away, and sat astride him.

'Look, Stan,' I said breathlessly, 'we're in this together. No one's trying to doublecross you.'

'I'll kill you!' he screamed. 'You and Lindsay! You've cooked it up between you.'

After that I had no choice it was either me or him, and in the circumstances I'd rather it was him. While he squirmed beneath me, shouting and raving, a bright gleam of madness in his eyes, I crashed my fist down into his face, time and time again.

At length he stopped moving.

I got up cautiously. Nothing happened. I eased my weight off him, standing up, still watching him.

Even so, I almost missed the hand that snaked out to grab my ankle. Without thinking, I kicked out. My foot caught him under the chin, moving him several inches along the floor. His head snapped back, making his shoulders arch, and this time he lay still there was no doubt that he was going to stay that way for a while.

To make sure I got the gun from underneath him, wiped it clean with my handkerchief and tossed it into a half-open drawer near Bannen. When White came round that would make us equal. I could have made things more equal by keeping the gun, but that way there was too much chance that I might shoot him.

And I wasn't a killer.

Nor did I intend to become one.

Breathing hard, I looked down at White. It was obvious that he wasn't going to come round for a long time. Maybe whoever had planned all this had also arranged for the cops to come, and in that case there was no time to hang around waiting for White to recover. The best plan was to drag him out to the car, but it wasn't until I tried to move him that I realized how impractical that was.

By the time I'd dragged him into the passage I knew that it was going to delay me far too long. He may only have been small, but his dead weight was too much for me to manage on my own; after moving him for only a few feet I was sweating and breath was whistling down my nose.

Yet if I left him there, wouldn't the cops find him?

Maybe, but on thinking about it that

didn't represent as much risk to me as it might seem. The cops could come and find him, but whatever he babbled to them about me, there was no way of proving it. They could have their suspicions, they could question me, but in the final analysis it would be my word against his and there wouldn't be a thing they could do.

Besides, why should I save him from the cops?

I still hadn't forgotten his threat to kill Lindsay, and from that point of view the best place for him was in a police cell.

Leaving him lying in the doorway, still unconscious, I padded down the passage, towards the back door. Now, the silence didn't seem half so menacing. I reached the door, opened it carefully and peered out. There was no one in sight, apart from a tramp near the street lamp, scuffling hopefully through the contents of a litter bin which was fastened to the lamp. He was too interested in that to worry about a bloke coming out of a doorway, so I slipped into the street, banging the door after me so that it locked, even remembering to wipe the handle clean.

I hadn't taken more than a few steps before I felt ill. A few moments later I was violently sick in the gutter, while the tramp watched me, open-mouthed. Casually, he tossed a ball of newspaper from out of the litter bin at my head. It missed, and rolled round and round in the pale pool of light from the lamp, while I lay on the edge of the pavement, watching it, thinking of Bannen and Lindsay and death.

3

When I reached Lindsay's flat I could tell from looking up at her window that she had no lights on. I slammed the door of the hired car, locked it, and grinned faintly to myself. She might be in darkness, but I was ready to bet she wasn't asleep. Not knowing what we were planning that night. Like White and myself, she was too alive to the prospects of a double-cross to go to sleep.

I went up the stairs, along the passage and rang the bell.

Almost at once there was the sound of a bolt being drawn back, and then Lindsay's voice.

'Who's that?' She sounded breathless and nervous, and I wasn't surprised.

'It's me, Matt.'

Another bolt was pulled back. The lock made a faint snick as she took off the catch. She opened the door and I stepped inside, pushing her out of the way and kicking the door shut with my heel.

Lindsay stared at me. She was still fully dressed, and she had the strained, aged look, of someone who hasn't slept for a long time.

'Matt,' she said in a hoarse voice, catching at my sleeve as I went into the lounge. 'Matt, what's the matter?'

'For God's sake make me a drink.'

She made it mechanically. There was obviously no sign of forty thousand pounds about me, and as soon as we were sitting down she asked me again what was wrong.

'Everything,' I said. 'To put it bluntly, Bannen's dead and there's no sign of the money.'

She caught her breath. Some of her drink spilled over her hand but she ignored it, for her eyes were on my own bloodstained fingers.

'Have you — '

'Don't be stupid,' I broke in, guessing what she was going to say. 'I didn't kill him. I got that when White bit me.'

'Bit you?'

I explained to her what had happened

when we'd found that the money wasn't there.

'I had to do something,' I finished. 'He'd have killed me if I hadn't got him first.'

'He's not dead?'

I shook my head.

'I had to knock him out. He's still there.'

'Still there!' Her voice rose. 'Matt, are you mad? The police will turn up there and — '

'There was nothing else for it,' I said harshly. 'You didn't see the way he was carrying on, the look in his eyes. He wanted to kill me, Lindsay, there wasn't much doubt about that. And you.'

That got her.

'Me?'

I nodded.

'The shock of losing the money like that has turned his brain if you ask me. He thinks it's something that we've fixed up between us. He was going to kill me there, and then come here and kill you.'

She didn't know what to say to that. She took a sip of her drink and her hand was shaking so much that the glass rattled against her teeth.

'Do you think he'll still come?'

'I'm certain of it. That's unless the cops get him before he has chance.'

'Have you phoned the police?'

'What do you think I am?' I asked shortly. 'Stupid? The first thing White's going to do is give both our names to the cops.'

'Then why did you leave him there?' She was looking at me now as if I was the one who was stupid.

'Because I didn't know when they were going to turn up. It would have taken me a good while to get him out to the car, they could have come at any time, someone could have seen me. I thought it was safer to leave him, because there's still a chance that he might recover before they get there. It depends on how things have been arranged. And whatever he tells them, they can't prove anything.'

There was a short silence, and I could see that she was going over in her mind all that I'd said. She must have agreed with me because in the end she smiled.

It was a faint, tremulous smile, but still a smile.

'Who do you think did kill Bannen, Matt?'

'That's a leading question,' I said. 'It could have been White, working some ploy of his own. It could have been me, working some ploy of my own.'

I paused, but she didn't say anything.

'Or it could have been Calloran,' I went on. 'If it was him it isn't very likely that he'd leave him in his own club.'

'And there's no reason why he should take the money,' Lindsay said.

'He could have done it as a blind,' I suggested, 'but as no one knows about it, that's not very likely either.'

'So where does that leave us?'

'With Calloran's enemies,' I said. 'A man like that must have plenty of them. Maybe you've heard something while you've been there?'

She shook her head.

'Sure?' I asked her.

'I'm certain,' she said. 'There's no one who stands out, anyway. A lot of the small men didn't like him but there was

165

nothing they could do about him. In any case, they were nearly all too scared even to bother.'

I put down my glass very carefully on the tray. I lined it up with the centre of the long sides, and then tapped it carefully with my finger nail so that it was right in the middle of the tray. Then I left it and leaned back.

'That leaves us with one of the big boys who's got sense enough to keep quiet about what he's doing,' I said. 'In that case he's big enough to be as dangerous to us as he was to Calloran. Or it leaves us with you.'

'Me?' Her breath came quickly. 'What do you mean, Matt?'

'You knew that Stan White and me were going there tonight. If anyone could have involved a plot to implicate us, you could.'

Her amazement died away to disbelief.

'I think that you're the one who's mad, Matt,' she said, her voice still a little unsteady, probably from the news I'd brought. 'Why should I want to do that?'

'To get the money.'

'There are better ways than that.' Her smile became easier. 'I know how both of you feel about me. If I'd wanted to get money off either of you I don't think I'd have much trouble, would I?'

She had me there, and I wasn't surprised. I'd never seriously thought that she could have had anything to do with it, but it was a possibility I had to take into account. As she'd said, using the same argument that I'd used to White, if she'd wanted to doublecross us there were easier ways. It was far more likely that one of Calloran's enemies was the man we wanted, but finding him, and the money, was another thing altogether.

'You'd better get out of your flat,' I said, pushing that aside for the time being. 'If White comes gunning for you, I don't want him to find you here.'

She set down her empty glass next to mine on the tray and juggled them about so that they were still both in the centre.

'If you really want to know,' she said, 'I don't think there's any danger there.'

'Why not?'

'I know Stan better than you. You've never seen his temper before. He says and does a lot of things when he's mad that he doesn't really mean.'

'Does he?' I said heavily. 'That'd be just fine for me if he'd shot me, wouldn't it?' A thought struck me. 'Any idea where he got his gun?'

'He's got a lot of queer friends,' she said. 'Getting a gun wouldn't be any problem to him. He probably brought it in case Bannen turned nasty.'

'How long do these tempers last?'

'They vary.'

'So he could still come round here, looking for us?'

She shrugged.

'He might do. It depends how hard you hit him.'

'I hit him hard enough,' I said grimly. 'I'm still not happy about the thought of you staying where he can find you.'

'I'm not moving,' she said sharply. 'The way I work, people, club owners and so on, have got to be able to find me quickly. Changing my flat would mess things up for months.'

'They might be messed up for ever if White's in the wrong mood when he finds you.'

'Matt,' she said quietly, 'I can handle him. I know him better than you ever will.'

I could have stayed there all night tossing that argument back and forth, and lost in the end. I had more important things to do, though, and as she was so confident I decided to leave it.

'What are we going to do about this money?' I asked.

'Do you think you can find it? After all, there must be hundreds of people who could have taken it.'

'There might be on the surface, but if we go into it I reckon we'll find that we can narrow it down,' I said. 'What I want you to do is think back over the past few weeks and see if you can remember anything that might be connected with it. It mightn't even be anything very much. Just a scrap of conversation, something concerning Calloran that might fit in now.'

'You're asking a lot, Matt,' she said. 'I

hear dozens of bits of conversation every night.'

'There's forty thousand pounds in it, don't forget,' I said sharply. 'It's worth remembering.'

'I know that, but it doesn't help me. Not on top of what's happened tonight.' She leaned forward and rubbed her hands over her face. 'Matt, for God's sake, there's too much happening. I feel as if I'm going out of my mind.'

She was sitting on the settee. As her voice rose towards the end of what she was saying I got up and went over to her, sitting down next to her. She leaned towards me, and I put my arm round her.

'Matt, can't you help me?' she cried, pressing herself against me. 'I haven't slept properly since this first started, long before Stan decided to bring you in on it. I can't think anymore, I can hardly remember what I'm supposed to be doing from day to day.'

'Take it easy,' I said. 'There's no hurry.'

Not much there wasn't, but the more she tried to force herself the less she was likely to remember.

She rubbed her hands over her face.

'It needn't have been at the Spanish Egg,' I went on. 'It could have been at one of Calloran's other clubs.'

'It could have been anywhere. That's what makes it so hopeless, Matt.'

We sat there for a minute or two. I could tell that she was trying to think, but she didn't seem to be getting anywhere. After a moment or two I got up and walked over to the drinks cabinet.

'Maybe another drink will calm you down a bit,' I said. 'If you can't remember anything after that we'll have to try something else.'

I was pouring the drinks when we heard a car stop in the car park outside. My thoughts immediately jumped to White, but I had the hired car and there hadn't been time for him to go home and get his own. Besides, after that kick I'd given him I didn't think he'd be in much condition to drive.

'There aren't many cars come here at this time,' Lindsay said nervously.

That was the thought in my own mind. Carefully I pulled back a corner of the curtain so that I could see out without much risk of being seen myself.

Parked down below was a police car.

A cop was just slamming the door, and looking up towards me.

* ★ ★

He hadn't seen me. I was fairly sure of that as I hastily let the curtain fall and stepped back to the centre of the room. Something of my alarm must have shown in my face, for Lindsay stood up, her arm raised as if she was already trying to ward off some unknown evil.

'Who is it, Matt?'

'The cops,' I said shortly. 'Is there any way out of this building other than by the front door?'

She hesitated for so long that I felt like grabbing her and shaking her.

'Well?' I growled. 'Is there?'

'I'm trying to think, Matt,' she screamed. 'Will you shut up! I wish I'd never started this, I wish — '

'You'll wish a lot more things if the cops find me here. They must have got

172

White and he's told them this is where I'll most likely be. If they don't see me I might be able to bluff my way out of it when they do catch up with me.'

All the time we were talking I kept imagining that cop climbing the stairs, getting nearer and nearer to the flat, cutting off any chance of escape that I might have. In spite of what I'd just said to Lindsay I didn't intend to let them get near me once I was out of here.

Though how I was going to achieve that wasn't too clear in my mind.

After what seemed an age Lindsay spoke.

'There's a fire exit,' she said, 'but I don't know if it's open.'

'It's not much use if it isn't. Where is it?'

'At the end of the passage,' she said, speaking quickly as if she'd at last realized the urgency of the situation. 'There's a door set flush with the wall. I think it comes out in the hallway downstairs.'

'That'll do me.'

I reached up to open the front door, but as I turned the knob Lindsay grabbed my arm, half swinging me round so that I was facing her.

'Matt,' she said, looking up at me, 'you'll be careful, won't you? If the police have got Stan I'm relying on you. Ring me up soon, won't you?'

Roughly, I shook her off, and opened the door.

'If I don't get out soon I'll be ringing you up from jail,' I growled. 'For God's sake let me get out before that cop comes.'

Before stepping into the passage I poked my head round the edge of the door. There was no one in sight, and with a reassuring grin to Lindsay I stepped out. Faintly now, I could hear the tread of footsteps on the stairs. The fire staircase would be at the opposite end of the building, of course, and, turning that way I began to hurry. Not enough to be noticed, but sufficiently fast to get me out of the way of the cop.

Lindsay's door closed. The snap of the lock was like an explosion in the silence of the night; I wished that I'd told Lindsay to get ready for bed as fast as she could, but it was too late now. All I could do was hope that she'd have the sense to realize that in the circumstances it would be suspicious if she were fully dressed at two o'clock in the morning.

I was so busy thinking about that, and wondering what kind of story she would put over to him, that I nearly missed the door. I spotted it then, nothing fancy, just a flat slab of wood let into the wall, with a scratched and faded sign screwed to it saying 'Fire Door'.

I turned the handle, wondering what would happen if someone had been stupid enough to leave it locked.

They hadn't.

It was a little stiff from disuse, but that was all.

I stepped into the blackness. There was a faint glimmer of light from the passage, but as soon as I closed the door after me that vanished, and I was in total darkness. Hardly daring to move in case I fell I shuffled forward, slapping the wall at the same time, trying to find a light switch. If there was one I couldn't put my hand on it. Maybe the planners had left it out. The thought of a pushing, shrieking crowd of people fleeing from a fire and thrusting down a pitch dark flight of stairs probably hadn't occurred to them. It occurred to me now as I blundered about trying to find out where the steps started, whether there was a bend in the passage, little things like that. Once I nearly fell. If I hadn't managed to save myself I would probably have gone head first to the bottom and broken my neck; the thoughts of that made me break out into a cold sweat.

Eventually my groping hands touched something right in front of me. Wood. There was a crack all round the edge. It must be the door at the bottom, and I paused, getting my breath and feeling for the handle. When I found it I turned it very slowly, pulling the door open inch by inch, moving my head until I could peer through the crack.

I'd expected that there'd be another cop in the hall.

What I hadn't expected was that he'd be looking straight at the door.

My natural reaction when I saw him

was to slam the door, but it was obvious from the way he was staring that he'd spotted someone was there. He hesitated just a fraction too long, giving me time to make up my own mind. If I'd closed the door I'd have been trapped; as it was, I could fling it open, jump out and through it and race across the hall.

The cop moved then.

He came at me as if his promotion depended on catching me. I swerved towards him without slackening speed and aimed a punch at his face. He flinched away, helped by a push in the chest from me, and then I was at the door, the night air striking chill and fresh against my face after the centrally heated warmth inside.

Where should I run?'

There was little point in circling back to the car park, trying to reach the car, because there would probably be more cops round there. Even if there weren't, by the time I'd got the door open and the engine started they'd be nearly on me. and it would be too easy for them to block my exit by swinging their own car across it. All I could do was pound across the street and down another side street, my only concern being to lose the sound of footsteps behind me.

Then I remembered the wood.

Lindsay's flat was quite a way out of London, and on one of my trips there I'd noticed there was a wood not far away. I'd never been in it but I reckoned that if I could once reach it I'd soon lose the cops, amongst the trees. They'd have a hard job following me through a wood in daylight, let alone at night.

All I had to do was hold them off until I reached it.

With the prospect of safety not far away I increased my speed, gasping for breath, ignoring my aching muscles and the pain which was starting to come in my side. The wood. I had to reach the wood, whatever happened. I'd be safe then, hidden where no cops could reach me, able to plan my next move.

And it would want some planning; I knew that without thinking about it.

Vaguely at the back of my mind I wondered what Lindsay was telling that cop who'd called at the flat, then I forgot about it. I had my own problems and it was going to take me all my time to solve them.

I risked a quick glance over my shoulder. I could see two men coming after me. One of them was dangerously close, and as I tried to increase my speed still further, my legs working like pistons but not seeming to get me anywhere, I heard him shout.

'You there! Grant!'

So they knew my name. It must have been White who'd given them that, and if that was so, what had he said about Lindsay? Probably quite a lot, but she struck me as a girl who'd keep her wits about her when she had to; you don't get on in the kind of world in which she moved by being stupid and dull. Provided she kept her head there was no reason why she shouldn't bluff her way out of it, either by telling them that I'd called there and she'd sent me away, or that White was someone she'd rejected and who was using this means of getting his own back. She'd be able to think of something, and in any case she hadn't actually been at the club and no one could prove she had.

All it needed was one fingerprint of mine in the wrong place at the Spanish Egg and I'd be right in the hot seat.

That was why I had to reach the wood, why I had to have time to sort out my thoughts, and to evolve some plan.

Across the road now I could see the trees, gaunt and black against the night sky. Running along the edge of this part of the wood were pointed iron railings; it would take too long to climb them and get in that way, so I swerved along the street, towards an entrance which I'd seen not far away.

I heard the cops swerve too, and out of the corner of my eye I saw one take a different line, crouching as he ran, his arms working away as he strove to get just that little bit in front of me to cut me off.

If he managed it I might as well give up.

With White, and probably Calloran, against me I'd be fingered for Bannen's murder without a doubt.

He didn't manage it.

We reached the gateway together. I raised my arm as I got there, pretending to fling something in his face. As he swayed to get out of the way of it he fell, staggering headlong, getting in the way of the other cop while I slipped past.

Before they'd recovered I was lost in the darkness of the wood.

It was eerie, but I wasn't worried about that. Faintly, I could hear the rustling of the leaves, the occasional creak of a branch. When I looked upwards the sky was criss-crossed by a delicate tracery of branches and twigs, with a few stars showing here and there, where the trees weren't growing quite so close together. I stumbled along a track, not sure where I was heading, not really caring so long as the cops didn't come with me.

At length I stopped for breath. There was no sound now, no sign of the cops. I leaned against a tree, listening carefully to make sure that I was alone, then I went on my way, walking normally now instead of hurrying and risking a fall. Presently the track led onto a fairly wide lane, and as I came out onto it I grinned for the first time since we'd set off to the Spanish Egg, seemingly years ago.

Parked at the top of the lane was a van.

It wasn't until I was quite close to it that it struck me it might be a police van. I stopped walking then and moved into the shadows. It didn't look as if it belonged to the cops but you can never tell these days. As I drew nearer I could see that it was too old and battered, and in any case there was no one in it. This was a lovers' lane kind of spot; whoever owned the van must have come here for an early morning drive and decided to go for a walk in the woods. That was all right by me. They were going to have a longer walk than they'd bargained for.

Providing I could open the driver's door, that was.

It's amazing how careless some people are. Not only was the door unlocked, but the ignition key was in the dash, catching the moonlight and gleaming bright silver.

I was still grinning as I turned it. The battery made heavy going of turning over a rather sluggish engine but it managed it at last. Gently I let in the clutch, knowing that if I stalled there might not be enough juice to start again; for the same reason I didn't put on the lights yet. They weren't really needed as there was enough moonlight to drive by, and with the state of that battery I wanted to put some of the charge back before I tried anything fancy.

Because of that I didn't see the bloke until it was almost too late. He was right in front of me, mouth open, yelling, arms waving, and he was making it pretty clear that it was his van. Just before I would have knocked him down he jumped back, and when I tried to pick him up in the rear-view mirror I couldn't see a thing. At first I thought that was because of the darkness, but then I realized that the van was closed in, the back part entirely separated from the cab.

Vaguely I wondered why the bloke had been on his own, then I shrugged. It was nothing to do with me. I had enough to do controlling the van as it lurched and bumped over the rutted lane, and wondering what I was going to do now. The obvious thing was to go to my flat, but it was more than likely that the cops would be waiting for me there.

After a couple of minutes I rounded a sharp bend in the lane and saw the lights of a road ahead. Accelerating slowly I travelled along the last few hundred yards of the lane. As I came to the end I saw something that I hadn't noticed before. A layby. Parked in the layby was a cop car and as the van ran onto the tarmac a couple of cops hurried out from the side, one of them with his hand raised.

The cop car began to back towards me.

The van gave a final lurch. The partition behind me slipped to one side, and in the driving mirror I could see the face of a girl. She looked towards me, and a sudden expression of fear came into her eyes.

It wasn't that which startled me, nor even the rag which was tied round her mouth.

It was the fact that she appeared to be naked.

★ ★ ★

The cop was very close. The stupid punk had his arm up as if he thought that he was back on point duty and I was bound to stop. As I drew up to him his mouth opened but before he had chance to say anything I slammed the van into second gear and trod on the accelerator. He jumped back. There was a faint slithering sound as if the van had grazed him as it passed. Either that or he slipped, because the last sight I had was of him sprawling in the roadway.

The Panda car was still backing out, turning round so tightly that I heard a faint squeal from the tyres.

In the mirror I could see the staring eyes of the girl.

There was no time to worry about her. All I wanted to do was get away from the cops. I was on the main road now, still with my lights out, and I kept the accelerator on the floorboards for as long as I dared, praying that the brakes would take it when I tried to slow down or stop, and that they weren't as ropey as the battery. They worked, but only just. Applying them had about as much effect as scraping my foot along the road would have done, but I managed to get round the corners without too much trouble, the cops dropping further and further behind.

It was a wild drive but eventually I lost them. As soon as I was sure that I was clear I stopped and switched off the engine. I hadn't much idea where I was, but it was a fairly lonely road and just the place for a talk with the girl. I got out and opened the back doors. I'd been wrong when I'd thought that she was naked; she had on a bra and skirt. Her blouse was over on the far side of the van. The rag was still in her mouth, and her arms had been fastened to the side of the van, above her head.

She watched me as I got in and closed the door after me.

Carefully I unfastened the cloth. It wasn't tied as tightly as I'd thought, nor, when I looked more closely, were her arms. Just enough to stop her from getting free. I undid the knots then tossed her blouse to her. She pulled it over her head and I said:

'Who the hell are you?'

She gave a muffled laugh, then settled the blouse and patted her hair.

'I'm the one who should be asking that question,' she said, not looking so scared now. 'You've stolen my boyfriend's van.'

'Boyfriend? And he leaves you like that?'

'It's a game,' she said.

I shrugged.

'One kink is as good as another. If you're both into the same bag I don't see that it matters. Is he the punk who tried to stop me when I was driving away?'

'I couldn't see him,' she said sullenly.

'A big guy. I didn't see much of him. He seemed upset about something.'

'That'll be Nobby,' she said confidently. 'He's always upset about something or other.'

'He'll be upset now,' I said grimly. 'What's the next move?'

She stared at me.

'Suppose we forget about that and you tell me what you're doing. When we've found that out — '

'I'm telling you nothing,' I said. 'The best thing you can do is clear off.'

'Clear off?' She was staring at me. 'You mean walk?' I nodded.

'But we're miles from anywhere!'

'So?'

'You can't just leave me here.' Some of the fear was coming back into her eyes. 'It'll take me hours to walk to somewhere I can get home from.'

She was right. I knew that the best thing to do was dump her, but yet I couldn't bring myself to leave her there, stranded, with no hope of a lift.

If she decided to stay of her own accord, that would be different.

'Look, kid,' I said, putting a rough note into my voice, 'it isn't safe to stay with me. The cops are after me. You probably saw them back there. If they catch up with me there's no telling what they might do to make me stop. You could get hurt.'

That was one of the things which was puzzling me about her. I'd stolen the van, and she must have guessed that the cops hadn't tried to stop me for that, yet she didn't seem bothered. From the calm way she was taking this we might have been any couple out for a Sunday afternoon picnic.

'The cops won't do anything that's dangerous,' she said, with the confident air of someone who knows. 'They don't work like that.'

'I might hurt you myself.'

She shook her head. Her pale face wagged from side to side in the darkness of the van.

'If you'd been going to hurt me you'd have done it by now, instead of sitting here talking.'

'Look, kid, I'm not going to tell — '

'And don't call me kid!' she flared suddenly, screaming the words out so that they echoed around the van. 'My name's Sally.'

'Listen, Sally — '

'Why are the cops after you?' she asked.

'It's nothing — '

'I'd like to know, Perhaps I can help you.' She looked at me smiling, and there was something about the smile which got right inside me. I don't mean that it was a pretty smile or anything like that. It wasn't. There was something simple in it, something creepy and awful which made me think that maybe she wasn't quite right in the head. That would explain her calmness too; probably she thought I was simply a nice man who'd come to take her for a drive in Nobby's van, while Nobby went picking flowers in the wood.

'Maybe I could help you,' she repeated, still smiling. I looked away, trying not to shiver. She was all right now, but what would happen in a couple of minutes if I didn't let her help me? I'd heard about people like her. If she really was mad she was likely to get violent if I crossed her, and that could lead to anything.

No wonder she wasn't worried.

All the signs now were that I was the one in danger, not her.

'I'd like you to help me, Sally,' I said, thinking quickly, 'but there are one or two things that I want to try and work out for myself first. I'm going to drive on for a mile or two.'

'I'll sit with you, shall I?' She moved closer to me, and I couldn't stop myself from cringing away.

'I drive better when I'm on my own,' I

said quickly. 'Having you next to me would only distract me.'

'I'll bet it would.' Her light laugh did nothing to ease my mind, nor did the way she tried to follow me when I slipped out of the back of the van.

'Stay there,' I said sharply.

'I want to come with you.'

'I've told you why you can't.'

'I don't believe you,' she said. 'You're only saying that because you don't want me.'

'Look, Sally,' I said, 'if there's any more of this nonsense I'm going to have to get rough.'

She giggled. That was another spine-chilling sound which made me hop quickly down into the roadway my hand on the van door.

'I like men who get rough,' she was saying, but I wasn't listening any more. As I slammed the doors her voice was cut off. When I got into the driving seat I caught a glimpse of her in the mirror again, staring at me, not moving, her eyes huge and round, only her head visible above the partition.

When I looked at that more closely I found that it was an amateur contraption and not particularly well-fitting, which explained why it had slipped. Even so, it was there and it would serve to stop the girl from getting at me.

I was sure she was a little crazed.

Either that or she was putting on a damned good act for some reason of her own.

Not that I really cared about that. All I wanted to do was get rid of her, and as soon as we reached the outskirts of the next town I was going to leave her, dump the van as close by as I could and somehow get back home. Now that the cops had seen me in it the van was a liability, but it would serve as transport for a few more miles.

I drove on, keeping a wary eye on the mirror in case the girl tried anything funny. From time to time I wondered about her boyfriend, Nobby, and what he was doing; then I had to push him to the back of my mind. The road wasn't a good one for speed, and it was taking me all my time to watch that and the girl and worry about my more immediate problems.

Who had killed Bannen? Where was the forty thousand? Had the cops got White, and how much had he told them? At the time running from Lindsay's flat had seemed the right thing to do but now I wasn't so sure. It could be that White had said so much that they'd arrested her as an accessory; in that case things wouldn't be too good.

As if that wasn't enough there was Calloran himself. I didn't know whether or not he'd been informed of what had happened yet, but the one thing that was certain when he did know was that he wouldn't sit back and leave everything to the cops. He wasn't that type. I could reckon on having him after me as well, and with his system of contacts it wasn't going to be very long before he found me.

I had to have a good story ready by then.

All this was in my mind as we swung round a corner. Too late I saw that there was a rabbit running across the road. As soon as it moved I swerved instinctively. The van rocked over onto two wheels before running off the road and onto the grass verge. I swung on the wheel again but it made no difference. There was a shrieking and grinding of metal as we hit the low stone wall at the side of the road, then the van tipped forwards as the front wheels dropped into a ditch.

Everything seemed to spin around me. My hands slapped against the windscreen, pawing at it, trying to save me from pitching headlong through it.

I felt an intense blow across my head, and then the glow of dawn in the sky was replaced by a widening spiral of light, right inside my head.

Suddenly it was gone and there was nothing.

The last thing I remembered was the hysterical, shrieking laughter of the girl in the back.

4

All this has taken me a long time to tell you, much longer than it took me to remember it, sitting in that transport cafe with the pop music paper in my hand, the truck driver looking at me oddly and the mugs of tea steaming unheeded on the table in front of us.

Suddenly the truck driver leaned forward so that he could see the paper I was reading. His eyes flickered over it, settling on the photograph; when he looked up at me a moment later there was a satisfied expression on his face.

'You look a lot like him,' he said flatly.

'I guess I do. That's what startled me.' I tried a laugh but it wasn't very good. 'I thought it was a picture of me at first.'

'I'd say it was,' he declared, looking at me more closely than ever. 'I'd definitely say that it was.' He turned and beckoned to the man behind the counter. 'Hey, Frank, have you got a minute?'

Frank nodded and started to come from round the counter. I felt trapped. In another few seconds these two would have established who I was. I didn't know what the papers had been saying about Bannen's murder, or even if they'd connected me with it, but staying around to find out could be dangerous.

By now Frank had reached the table. He wiped his hands on the front of his apron, and looked enquiringly at the truck driver.

'What can I do for you, Bob?' he asked.

'Who would you say this was?' Bob demanded, pointing to the photo. 'Would you say it was this bloke here?'

'If you'll excuse me,' I said, standing up and knowing that I was settling the argument by my actions, 'I'll be on my way.'

'You've a bloody long walk in front of you if you go now,' Bob said with a chuckle. 'Must be ten miles at least. You'd better wait for me.'

Frank was looking at the picture, staring at it, then at me and finally nodding, wiping his hands again.

'It's him.'

'I thought so.'

Apart from us there was only one chap in the cafe, and he was staring across by now, obviously after something to brighten up the boredom of his normal life and hoping that I would oblige by causing some kind of trouble.

'How come you're hitching a lift?' Bob, the truck driver, asked. 'I thought that all you pop singers were rolling in money.'

I shrugged.

'Some are, some aren't. I'm one of the ones that isn't.'

As I spoke I knew that it wasn't a very good answer, and that it would take a lot more to satisfy him. Worse, there was a shrewd look in his eyes, and even if there'd been a picture of me in the paper in connection with the killing there was no guarantee that he'd give away the fact that he knew that was me too. He could string me along for some time and then hand me over to the next copper we saw.

Sweat was beading my forehead as I tried to look as though I was unconcerned.

'Surely you can afford a car of some sort?' the truck driver was insisting. 'Or at least the train fare. You don't have to go about begging lifts, do you?'

'I've got a car,' I said, struggling to think of some reasonable explanation. Suddenly I had a brainwave. 'Look,' I went on, 'keep it quiet will you? There's already someone looking at us.'

Both Frank and the truck driver turned to look at the man who was watching us. He wasn't abashed in any way but continued to stare back as if he was in a trance.

'You don't mind that, do you?' Frank asked. 'I thought that all you people wanted was publicity.'

'Not in this case.' I kept my voice low, partly so that the bloke across the cafe wouldn't hear what I was saying and partly so that Frank and Bob would have to concentrate on my words and wouldn't have time to work out anything else, or question them. 'My publicity agent has sent me a bill. I'm saying that he's no good. I told him that I could travel fifty miles and not be recognized. He said I couldn't but if I'm right he's going to cut his bill.'

I was hoping that they wouldn't spot the obvious flaws in this. The truck driver seemed satisfied, but Frank frowned then said:

'How's he going to know that you haven't been recognized? In any case, you have.'

'But only because of that photograph,' I said, passing off the first question. 'And that's something I arranged myself when I hadn't even heard of this bloke.'

Frank shrugged.

'It still sounds queer to me but I suppose you know what you're doing.'

The article was one which I remembered now, the last one in a series about so-called forgotten pop stars; it wasn't a very flattering way to be written about but I hadn't had much choice and at that time anything was better than nothing. All the time I was talking to Frank and Bob I was expecting them to ask why it said that I'd gone out of favour, but either they hadn't read it or they didn't care.

I was still glad when I got outside again.

As we climbed into the truck Bob said: 'Where shall I drop you?'

'Anywhere so long as I can get back to London.'

Dawn had broken by the time I left him, at a tiny railway station which he assured me was still open. It was, but only just. I found out that I'd an hour to wait for a train, and then I'd have to change a few miles down the line, but at least I was on my way back now.

While I was waiting I had time to think. I could remember everything with a clarity that was in startling contrast to the earlier fog. The only thing I wasn't sure about was how Sally and Nobby had come to know so much; eventually I realized that I must have been unconscious for a while, babbling away like someone talking in his sleep. Even though I hadn't been able to remember anything about them, events must have been preying on my mind, and it was natural that I'd talk about the murder and the forty thousand pounds.

Had I talked about Lindsay?

I must have done, because Nobby had said something about her when he'd thought that I was only fooling him.

How much more had I said? Had I give away my address? Had I mentioned Calloran, a name that would probably mean nothing to him but which could cause plenty of trouble for me if Nobby started following it up? There were so many things I could have given away, and I had no way of knowing what I'd actually said.

That could make things very difficult, but it paled into nothing beside another thought which I had.

Would the cops be watching my place?

That was highly likely, and if they were I was going to be in worse trouble than ever.

I didn't have to wait long to find out the answer to that. By the time the train had come and I'd wended my way into London newspapers were on sale. I bought one, feeling scruffy and out of place in the tight jeans and bulky sweater which I was still wearing, but no one seemed to take much notice.

According to the date on the paper it was nearly a week since Stan White and I had found Bannen dead; if I'd been away for so long there was a good chance that a lot of the urgency would have gone out of everything, and that maybe the cops would have assumed that I'd gone for good.

It wasn't much to hope but it was something, and in the event it was right.

There wasn't any sign of them around my flat.

I took my time before I went in, approaching from all angles, making sure that no one was hiding, feeling more like a thief than a home-coming boy. When cops are watching a place they tend to stand out; I'd learned that much during my singing days when our parties were often watched for signs of drug activities. Only when I was certain as I could be that everywhere was clean did I go into the building and up to my flat.

If they got me here I'd probably be trapped. That was why I'd taken such care.

It had never occurred to me that there might be anyone in my flat itself. I saw him as I closed the door and snapped down the light switch, a biggish bloke, sitting front-to-back on one of my wooden kitchen chairs, placed in the middle of the wreckage and shambles of what had once been a reasonably clean and tidy living room.

My eyes went from the mess to the gun which he was resting on the back of the chair.

'Hi Grant,' he said with a smile. 'I think this is for you.'

He lobbed something at me across the room.

* * *

In the first flash of the movement I couldn't see what it was that he had thrown. It came at me gently, twisting and fluttering like a big, square snowflake against a background of the walls and ceiling. I stared at it, watching it fall, then made a clumsy movement and managed to catch it.

'What is it?' I asked him, my eyes held by the gun.

'Have a look and see. I won't shoot you. Not yet, anyway.'

It was a letter, addressed to me in a rounded, childish writing which I didn't recognize at all. With exaggerated care I tore it open, wondering if it was some kind of joke. It wasn't. It was a note from Canston, reminding me that I owed him two weeks' payment on the loan and asking me what I intended doing about it. From the tone of it I didn't have much difficulty in guessing that it was his thugs who'd wrecked the room, and that had I been here too they'd have wrecked me along with it.

I shuddered.

The cops. Nobby. Calloran. Canston. It seemed as though everyone was after me for one thing or another, but mainly for money. Nobby and Calloran for forty thousand quid, Canston for five and a half thousand. And me with a shade under two pounds in my pocket which I'd lifted from Nobby on my way out. But for the gunman who was staring at me blandly I could have laughed; as it was I crumpled the note into my pocket and looked back at him.

'Who the hell are you?'

'My name's Pardoe,' he said, dropping his head so that his chin rested on the back of the chair, just behind the gun, so that the end of the barrel looked as though it was his mouth, permanently screwed into a pinched O of astonishment, even while he was talking.

'So why have you come here?'

'I've come to see you, Grant,' he said. 'As a matter of fact I've been waiting a week for you, on and off. Pretty boring it's been. I'm ready for some action now.'

It was a question which had to be asked, though now I was afraid of the answer.

'Are you a cop?'

'No,' he said softly, shaking his head. 'I work for Mr Calloran.'

Somehow I'd been expecting that answer. Cops don't carry guns and they don't wait in people's flats. Even so, the words sent a chill along my back. It seemed to crawl up, right from the base of my spine, until it could grab the hairs on the back of my neck and ruffle them. Calloran. Once he got me I wouldn't have much of a chance

'What does he want?' I asked.

'Can't you guess?' Pardoe moved his head and I saw that he was grinning. 'He wants to know what's happened to his forty thousand quid.'

I gave what was meant to be a carefree shrug.

'No use asking me, pal. I've no idea.'

The smile faded from his face slowly. He wagged the gun at me, like a chiding finger of death.

'We think you do, pal. Anyway, it isn't me you've got to convince. It's Mr Calloran.'

'I don't need to convince anyone,' I said, making a weak attempt at a bluff. 'What I'm saying is the truth and there's no way of altering it.'

'There are are plenty of ways,' he said briefly, then nodded towards the phone. 'Dial this number.'

'Why?' I asked, interrupting him as he rattled it off.

His voice was still pleasant. But for the gun it would have been hard to tell that he was a thug, but that was the way Calloran ran his operations. Subtle and unobtrusive. Happy, amiable gunmen, well dressed in a green knitted casual jacket and green trousers. His overcoat was folded neatly over the back of an armchair.

'You'll dial it because if you don't you'll get a bullet in the leg. That won't stop you talking but it'll make things hard for you.'

'Does the phone still work?'

'They left you that,' he said with a nod. 'Presumably so that they could ring you if they wanted. Who were they?'

'You didn't see them?'

'It was like this when I came the other day,' he said. 'How about dialling that number?'

There didn't seem much choice in the matter. I crossed to the phone, stepping over a litter of broken and twisted records, a charred mass of what had once been clothes, the ashes still soggy from the water which had been poured over them, the television set shattered from where the bucket had afterwards been pushed through the screen.

I dialled slowly.

'When someone answers, tell them your name and say that you're ready,' Pardoe told me.

It seemed a little comic-opera to me, but it was as good a way as any of getting reinforcements. After the call, which produced no comment at the other end but the sound of rasping breath and a click, I set about clearing up as much as I could, while Pardoe watched me, occasionally asking questions about it, questions which I didn't answer in case they made matters any worse.

After all, owing Canston five and a half thousand pounds was a good reason for stealing forty thousand.

Soon there was a knock at the door. Pardoe sent me to open it. The man who stepped in, pushing me to one side, nodded to Pardoe.

'Lives in a pig sty, doesn't he?' he said sneeringly. 'No wonder he wanted Mr Calloran's money.'

'I haven't got Mr Calloran's money,' I said tightly.

'That doesn't surprise me. You've had a week to find a hiding place for it.'

I swallowed.

'I'll talk to Calloran,' I said. 'Maybe I can make him see sense.'

'Mr Calloran to you,' Pardoe said as we went out, while his pal slammed the door.

Calloran lived in the sort of house where I'd have expected to find him, a big place in North London set in its own grounds and approached by a sweeping, gravelled drive. I was sitting in the back of the car, between Pardoe and the other man who'd come into my flat; a third man was driving, and as we stopped outside the front door he said:

'Hurry up and get the punk inside. Mr Calloran's been waiting too long for him already.'

I was hustled into the hall, along a passage, through a doorway. Pardoe seemed to have changed in a subtle way since coming in here, his behaviour towards me hardening but his general manner tending the other way, not creeping, exactly, but as if he were already deferring to the expected arrival of Calloran.

Or should I say Mr Calloran?

I'd seen him before, when I'd been to the Spanish Egg. To look at there was nothing sinister about him, which was the secret of most of his success at keeping out of the way of the cops. He was sitting in a big armchair in a plush room now, with a colour television set in the shape of a big white sphere playing softly at one end. From where he was sitting he couldn't see the picture. Maybe he didn't want to. If someone had pinched forty thousand quid off me I wouldn't want to watch television either.

'Sit down, Mr Grant,' he said, watching me carefully. 'Drink?'

'Thanks,' I said. It was a veneer of civilization but I didn't let it fool me. The moment he thought he'd got everything possible out of me he'd tell his goons to kill me and that would be the end of it. I knew that, but I hadn't been able to think of a way out at all.

I sipped the drink. For all I knew it

could have been doctored.

'You know what I want,' he said. 'Are you going to talk now or make it hard for yourself?'

'I don't know anything,' I said. 'I've already told Pardoe that.'

Out of the corner of my eye I saw Pardoe moving round behind me, his feet sinking into the thick pile of the carpet. He disappeared from view. A moment later I felt the cold touch of the gun barrel against the back of my head.

I swallowed.

'Sure you don't know anything?' Calloran asked, his voice as cold as the steel.

'Not a thing.'

'Your name is being linked with the theft,' Pardoe said, 'How's that come about if you don't know anything?'

But for the gun I'd have given a careless shrug.

'Maybe it's someone with a grudge against me,' I said.

'Who could that be?'

'I don't know.'

'There must be someone who doesn't

like you. In the pop business I'd have thought you'd have plenty of chance to make enemies.'

'Not that kind of enemy.' A thought struck me about the drift of his questioning. 'How do you know I didn't do it myself?'

'I don't,' Calloran said, 'but I'm assuming it because I've never heard of you. If you were big enough to organize a steal like that I'd know all about you. I'd have made you an offer before now.'

He seemed to think that was a reasonable assumption. He also had the impression that because of what I knew I'd spent the past week hiding, even though I insisted that I'd been staying with a friend.

I could have told him about White. I could have mentioned Nobby and Sally and Doc Kyme, but I wanted to keep everything to myself for so long as I could. There was Lindsay to think of, too; I didn't even know what the cops had said to her that night, years ago it seemed.

In my mind I was being drawn more and more to the theory that White had somehow doublecrossed me. If he'd got the money beforehand, and then come in with me knowing that Bannen was dead, it sounded bizarre on the face of it, but there was a simple explanation.

By pretending rage he could allay my suspicions.

Then, by knocking me out and leaving me there, he could use me as a scapegoat.

To me there was nothing simpler, and it explained everything, even how the cops had turned up at Lindsay's. The only doubt was whether or not I'd ever get chance to test my theories; even if Calloran didn't kill me it wasn't likely that White would have hung around for a full week. He'd be well clear by now, probably having persuaded Lindsay to go with him.

Calloran was still talking, questioning insistently, while I stubbornly stuck to my denials. Gradually I could tell that the meeting was drawing to a close, even though I was actually trying to spin it out, hoping that something would happen which would save me from the inevitable bullet.

'Look,' Calloran said finally. 'I've lost forty thousand pounds. Why not — '

'Why not call the police in?' I asked. 'Why go to all this trouble?'

'I don't want to involve the police,' he said. 'That's as good a reason as any as far as you're concerned.'

I didn't press him because I didn't want to make it look like I knew too much about his affairs. Dimly I'd thought that there might be an out there, but if I was wrong I'd have to leave it.

Pardoe was still holding the gun against my head.

I could almost imagine his finger tightening on the trigger.

'Why not co-operate?' Calloran said. 'It'd be much easier for everyone.'

'I can't co-operate, because I don't know anything. Can't I drive that into your thick head?'

Speaking to Calloran like that was a bit like slapping the face of a cop who's just booked you for parking, but if I was going to be shot I might as well make the most of it. In a detached sort of way I regretted that I wouldn't be around to see what sort of mess my brains made on his lovely thick carpet, but just then he said something that made it look as though the problem wouldn't arise.

'Take him out.'

The words had an abruptly final sound about them. The pressure of the gun against my head eased and I started to lunge forward, striking at Calloran in a desperate attempt to break away before I was killed. Calloran had an amused smile on his face. I should have known that he was too far away for me to reach him, and even as I moved Pardoe grabbed hold of my collar, yanking me backwards, tightening his grip so that I was strangling.

Much less messy than a bullet.

He swung me round, out of the chair, twisting me so that I could see how he was grinning at me.

'Come on, punk,' he said. 'Time to go home.'

Home?

He thrust me towards the door.

'If you remember anything, Grant, let me know,' I heard Calloran say as I was pushed out.

'Get a move on,' Pardoe snarled into my ear. 'He might change his mind about leaving you alive.'

It didn't take much more than that to move me. Pardoe helped me down the steps by a push in the back which sent me staggering forward until my hands banged against the side of the car, making a metallic slapping sound.

Ten minutes later I was on my own, pushed out of the car in a quiet side street, reminded of Calloran only by the roar of the engine as the car moved away, and the memory of Pardoe's laughter as I'd fallen into the gutter. I was quite a way from home but at least I was alive. As soon as I got back I was going to clean myself up, and then phone White's flat. If I was right, and he had got the money, there'd be no answer, either there or at his office.

If I was wrong —

It was going up for lunchtime when I finally called him. No one was more surprised than me when he answered.

★   ★   ★

We didn't talk much on the phone. I had a lot of questions I wanted to ask him, but he cut me short, telling me that it would be better if I came round to his flat.

'Sure you'll still be there when I arrive?' I asked sourly.

'Why shouldn't I be?'

'I can think of forty thousand reasons why you shouldn't be,' I said. 'Where's Lindsay?'

'She'll be here too,' he answered, and I could tell from the tone of his voice that he knew that would stop any further argument from me.

It did. I hurried round, working myself up into a fine rage on the journey, convinced that he had the money and that this was some other form of trickery.

Yet if he had it, and Lindsay was with him now, it surely meant that she was involved with him. And if that was the case, why send the cops to her flat after me? The more I thought about that the less it added up, but I didn't worry overmuch. White would soon give me the answers when I got to work on him.

Things weren't so simple as that. The

inevitable row developed as soon as he opened the door, continuing through the hall and into the lounge, where Lindsay was sitting in the middle of the yellow dragon rug, picking nervously at it with her finger. She looked up when she heard my voice, and gave me a faint smile.

'Where have you been, Matt?' she asked.

I didn't answer her. I was too busy yelling at White, he yelled at me, both of us slowly becoming convinced that the other was telling the truth.

'All right,' I said finally, sitting down, 'let's call it a day. If you haven't got the money and I haven't got it, who has?'

'I can think of one or two.'

'Such as?'

His gaze turned to Lindsay.

'You've got a lot of queer boyfriends, Lindsay. Are you sure you didn't mention it to one of them?'

I could tell from her weary expression that this was a line he'd taken before, while I'd been away.

'Why should I do that?' she asked. 'There'd be no point to involving two of you, would there? Maybe Calloran got wind of what we were going to do and shifted the money somewhere else.'

'Calloran?' he repeated. He made it sound like one of those magic words which the Indians use as a chant.

I shook my head.

'I've just come back from a talk with Calloran,' I said. 'It's safe to say that he doesn't know anything about it. He thought I had the money.'

'How did he know about you?'

I shrugged.

'The same way that the cops knew I was at Lindsay's that night,' I said. 'What happened then? I thought you must have told them.'

'They didn't get me,' he said. 'It was a miracle, because I was only just coming round when they got into the building. I managed to avoid them, and they didn't even see me.' His voice hardened. 'I thought that you must have sent them.'

'They wouldn't tell me anything,' Lindsay put in before I could speak. 'All they could say was that they wanted to speak to you and they'd heard that you were in my flat.'

'What did you tell them?'

'That you'd called and asked me to hide you. I'd refused and you'd run off.' She gave another faint smile. 'What else could I say?'

'Not much,' I agreed. 'Did they believe you?'

She nodded.

'I got the impression afterwards that they were chasing you and of course all that fitted in with what I'd just said. They haven't bothered me since, anyway, so I must be in the clear.'

'Has there been anything about me in the papers?'

'No one's been named, apart from Bannen as the dead man and Calloran as the owner of the club,' White said, 'so it looks to me as though the cops haven't much evidence of any kind.'

'That's something,' I said, relief evident in my voice. 'They aren't watching my place either.'

'They were up to a couple of days ago, but they must have decided by now that you're not coming back.' White gave a smile. 'The next thing they'll decide is that you must be the man they're after.'

'That's what worries me,' I said. 'And they aren't the only ones who're after me.'

As quickly as I could I told them about Sally and Nobby and Doc Kyme. I could almost hear the Doc's shrill giggling as I spoke, and even though there was no chance of his turning up here the thought of him could still send a shiver down my back. When I had finished, White and Lindsay sat there in a silence which went on for so long that I felt I had to say something else.

'Well?' I demanded. 'Haven't you any comments?'

'Not much we can say, is there? Any idea where to find these characters?'

'I don't want to find them. All I want to do is keep well clear of them. They're a complication I can manage without.'

'More important,' Lindsay said, 'do they know where to find you?'

'They might do,' I said slowly. 'I must have talked a lot while I was unconscious, because they know all about the money and Bannen, though they had the idea that I'd killed him. They knew your name, too.'

'Mine?'

I nodded, and she bit her lip, plucking at the rug again while the dragon leered up at her.

'One thing I can't understand,' White said, 'is why didn't Calloran have you killed when he'd finished with you?'

'That's the sort of question I thought it better not to ask him,' I said. 'I didn't want to start a discussion like that.'

Nevertheless, that was something which remained in my mind when I was on my way back from White's, our argument still unresolved, our questions about where the money had gone completely unanswered.

'Why had Calloran let me go so easily? The obvious answer was that he thought I might lead him to someone else. Such as White and Lindsay. I went cold at the thought of Lindsay falling into his hands but if he had had someone watching me it was too late to do anything about it now. Like a sucker I'd walked right into his trap, and there was nothing I could do to alter it.

It wasn't until later that I actually saw the man. I'd spent the time trying to clear up the ruin of my flat, and seeing what I could salvage from the debris, and it was when I finally put on the light and went over to draw the curtains that I noticed him, standing further along the street, not making it obvious that he was watching my flat but not leaving much doubt about it, either.

I pulled the curtains together and moved away, not surprised to find that sweat was streaming down my face. So Calloran still thought I had something to do with it. He'd sent this goon to keep an eye on me, and as soon as he was satisfied that I had no information he'd have me killed. I was under no illusion about that but I couldn't see anyway out of it, without involving the cops.

Which was the last thing I intended doing.

Somewhere, there was forty thousand pounds, and I wanted it. I had to find that money before Calloran could have me killed, and before the cops caught up with me.

But if White hadn't given my name to the cops and Calloran, who had? I still couldn't accept that Calloran's network of spies was so good that he could say at once who was responsible for every attempted robbery, even when it concerned himself. It wasn't as if I normally moved in criminal circles. There was no way in which he could have heard of me without being specially told.

Could Lindsay have told him? Doubts started to creep into my mind. But why should she go to all the trouble of getting me and White there at the club if she was going to go straight to Calloran afterwards? I couldn't figure out what was going on; all I knew was that before long I was going to be dead, unless I did something to throw off Calloran's man.

I didn't kid myself it would be easy. Calloran hadn't got where he was by making things easy for anyone.

The first thing was to get out of my flat, to go somewhere where it would be hard for anyone to find me again. With that as a base I could start looking round, poking into things, uncovering what I could until sooner or later I stumbled across something which would help me. Put that way it sounded very attractive, and I began to pack my things quickly. In a way I was lucky, because when Canston's thugs had been round here they'd destroyed pretty near everything; what was left went easily into a suit case, which I could carry without looking conspicuous. I was almost through when there came a ring at the doorbell.

I stiffened.

Maybe this was Calloran's man now. If he came in and found me with a suitcase packed he'd twig at once what was going on and that would be that. Working as fast as I could I took the case into the bedroom and slid it under the bed; if he made any comment about the bare appearance of the flat I'd have to pass it off somehow. When I'd done that I slipped over to the window, and wasn't surprised to see that Calloran's button man had gone.

More worried than ever now I opened the door just a crack, keeping a firm hold on it, ready to slam it if he tried anything funny.

The man standing outside was the one I'd seen watching earlier. He gave a bright smile, so bright that the edges of it were cut off by the narrowness of the crack through which I was looking.

'I'm glad you're back, pally,' he said. 'I want a word with you.'

'I've been back a long time,' I said stiffly, 'and in any case I've already said all I've got to say to Mr Calloran.'

The smile faded a little.

'Calloran?' he said. 'You mean the club owner? Who said anything about him?'

'I thought — '

'You think too much. I'm from Mr Cranston and I want to have a talk with you about all that money you owe him. We thought you'd run away so that you wouldn't have to pay him, pally.'

With that he raised one foot and kicked the door, knocking it right out of my grasp and leaving it wide open so that he could swagger into the flat.

Behind him was another man. He was holding a set of knuckledusters, and the hall light glinted on them as he polished them with his sleeve.

5

It was later that same evening when I went to see Marvin Freeman, the one person whom I thought might help me out of my troubles. I'd been to his place a couple of times before, during my better days. Then, I'd been making money for him as well as for myself and I'd been a welcome guest; I wasn't sure what kind of a reception I was going to get now, and because of that I hadn't phoned him beforehand.

I wanted to see him, and I wasn't going to give him chance to turn me away the easy way, over the phone.

When I'd first met him I'd expected that he'd live in a flat. I was quite wrong. He lived in a big house, the kind which the more affluent Victorians used to build for themselves, and which today are usually crumbling relics, converted into about a dozen flats, or scheduled for early demolition.

Freeman's was neither. It had been modernized, seemingly regardless of cost, providing ample indication for anyone who needed it of the kind of income which Freeman made as an agent. At first I'd thought that it must prove how good he was at managing the people whom he'd taken on; now, with the bitterness of own experience, I'd change my mind and say that it showed how well he knew how to milk his performers of every penny that he could get out of them.

As I rang the bell, hearing nothing but a faint bing-bonging echo from somewhere inside the house, I was feeling bitter against him, and against the way he'd dragged me from the life I'd known, and then tossed me away when I was no further use to him. It irked me to have to run to him now, but maybe that was a habit I'd fallen into during the days when all problems were referred to him automatically. As far as I could tell he'd done as much as anyone to produce this problem by dropping me, and it was up to him to help me solve it.

Besides, he'd introduced me to Cranston in the first place.

The door was so long in opening that I began to think he wasn't in. Either that or he was hiding for some reason. Just as I raised my hand to ring again there was the sound of a catch snicking back, and then the door opened.

It was Freeman himself, looking at me with a blank expression on his face as though he didn't recognize me. 'Hello, Marvin,' I said, sounding like the younger son in a Victorian novel, come home to roost at last.

He peered forward into the darkness.

'Matt! What are you doing here?'

'I've come to see you,' I said, a touch of irritation creeping into my voice. 'Aren't you going to ask me in?'

'Well — ' He broke off. 'What have you done to your face, lad?'

'It isn't what I've done. Other people did most of it.'

'Fallen under a bus? Or been mobbed by a crowd of fans?'

'Those days are over and you know it.' I was becoming more and more needled by the jeering note in his voice. 'If you must know, your pal Cranston sent a couple of thugs round to beat me up. I want to talk to you about it.'

'Nothing I can do, Matt. I'm sorry.'

I thought I detected a flutter of his hands, a slight tremor of movement to indicate that he was shutting the door. I wedged my foot into it.

'Are you asking me in, Marvin?' I said pointedly.

'If you insist, though I don't see what I can do.' He sounded most unhappy, and he looked it too, as he stepped back and opened the door wide enough for me to get in.

I followed him along the passage and into the lounge. A record was playing softly on the stereo. Not a pop record, so it couldn't be any connection with him, but something classical, obviously meant to be soothing. Over the restored fireplace was a mirror, and as I sat down, stiffly, I caught sight of myself in it.

No wonder he hadn't wanted to let me in. With my bruised and puffy face I looked more like an out-of-work boxer than a pop singer.

'Drink?'

I nodded. I could have used one before this, but I hadn't really the money to spare. Freeman poured them out and handed mine to me.

'What do you think I can do?' he asked, taking a sip of his own. 'I've no control over Cranston.'

'I thought he was a friend of yours.'

'He might be, but that doesn't mean I can order him about. All I do really is to give him a little business every now and then.'

'People you've blown up beyond their means and then ruined?'

'Matt — '

'You know the state of my finances,' I said, interrupting him. 'I blame it all on you. If you'd stood by me when things started to go down I wouldn't be in this mess now. Instead you kicked me out, left me to fend for myself, knowing how little money I had.'

'Matt,' he said soothingly, leaning against the fireplace, looking cool and at ease, 'is it my fault that the public went off you? Could anything that I might have done have altered that?'

'Maybe,' I said, 'but I'm not here to go into that. It's done now and there's no going back. What I want you to do is get your pal to call off his thugs.'

'I've already — '

'They burnt all my stuff and wrecked my flat,' I went on, 'and this afternoon they came and beat me up. That's why my face is in such a mess. That's why I can hardly move.' As I said that my face twisted in a spasm of pain. I couldn't avoid it, but it was a good thing because Freeman seemed to soften slightly when he saw it. To console himself he took another delicate sip of his drink, then he set the glass down on the wide mantel piece.

'Why did they do that, lad?'

'Because I'm a little behind with the payments.'

'How many?'

'Only two of them, Marvin.'

'And you want me to pay those two, to straighten you out?'

I shook my head. It was an effort

because my neck was still throbbing from where I'd been kicked as I lay on the burnt remnants of my carpet, already dazed and moaning with pain from being batted between the thugs like a ping-pong ball.

'I want him taking off my back,' I said. 'I can make all the payments, but I just need a little time. That's all. Time.'

'Canston doesn't like people who miss,' he said.

'I can pay him!'

'How?'

'Just give me time.'

Actually, I didn't want the time for that. I wanted it for keeping out of Calloran's hands while I searched for that money. Finding it would be a hard enough job under ideal conditions, let alone with a couple of thugs tailing me for something else. And they were tailing me. I'd managed to give them the slip tonight, but it had taken some doing, and I was half in fear of another beating when I got back home. Leaving my flat, as I'd originally intended, was equally impossible under those conditions, and sooner or later someone was bound to catch up with me.

Even if it was only the cops.

They were the least of my worries.

'Matt, there's nothing I can do,' Freeman said, his voice full of sorrow which he couldn't possibly have been feeling. 'I'd like to help you, but — '

'Marvin, I'm insisting that you help me.' I said savagely.

'How are you going to back up that threat?' His eyes narrowed as he spoke and one hand moved towards the reassuring drink, the symbol of respectability and calmness.

'I'm going to start right now, the way Canston's thugs started.' I half moved to get up, ignoring the pain in my back, but he put out his hand, not to fend me off, but as some kind of a warning. At the same time he glanced towards the door, which was opening slowly.

'Matt,' he said, 'your usefulness is long past and you're starting to be a nuisance.' He looked beyond me, and there was a sort of jeering expression on his face. 'Don't you think so, too?'

I half turned to see whom he was talking to.

The door opened fully, and Lindsay came into the room.

★ ★ ★

The thing which struck me most about her was the way that she looked at me, a sort of contemptuous, hard, indifferent expression, everything all mixed up in one, so that it was impossible to tell which emotion was dominant. I stared at her, then I said slowly:

'Is Marvin your agent?'

She nodded.

'He has been for a long time. I'm surprised that you never twigged the connection before now.'

The tone of her voice matched the look on her face. She came further into the room and went over to the drinks cabinet, deliberately moving in the sexy way she used on stage, showing me how unattainable she was.

'You planned this from the first, you and Marvin, didn't you?'

She poured herself a drink before answering, and then perched on the corner of the table.

'We didn't plan to involve you, not right at the start, anyway. It was only when you turned up at my flat, hawking those teddy-bears, that we included you.' She ignored the warning look which Freeman gave her. 'We needed a scapegoat, Matt, someone for Calloran to find when the money disappeared. You and Stan White were the perfect solution.'

I nodded.

'Of course we were. You heard about the money and plotted with Freeman to steal it.' I spoke slowly, working things out in my head as I went along. 'You knew that Calloran would launch a search, even though the cops wouldn't be involved. Once Calloran got going his network or spies and informers would soon ferret something out, and you knew that you wouldn't be safe for very long.'

'That's it. So I involved you and Stan. Calloran would find you, and while he was concentrating on getting you to tell him where you'd hidden the money we

237

could be well away.'

'But you spoiled it,' Freeman said. 'Typical of you, Matt, to mess things up. You went missing and we didn't dare make a move until you showed up again in case you'd worked it out and you were waiting for us to do something.'

I laughed. It was a short, barking sound, but it did a little to ease the knot of tension inside me.

'Who actually broke in?'

'I did,' Freeman said. 'I knew from Lindsay exactly what your plans were, and it was easy to forestall you.'

'And who killed Bannen?'

Freeman didn't answer. Instead he crossed swiftly to the sideboard and opened a drawer. When he turned back to face me, he was holding a gun. I knew instinctively that it was the gun which had been used to kill Bannen, and which would shortly be used to kill me.

'He got in the way,' Freeman said dreamily. 'I had some friends with me, helping me, and Bannen heard them. I had to kill him or the whole plan would have fallen apart.'

'It falls apart if you kill me,' I said, trying to keep the desperation out of my voice.

He shrugged.

'I shan't be around to care,' he said.

'Nor me,' Lindsay put in.

Freeman nodded, and the little smile on his face sent a chill through me. I thought that Lindsay hadn't realized what he had in mind, but suddenly she gave a gasp.

'Marvin — '

'Shut up,' he said roughly. 'You've had it coming for a long time, if only you'd known. You can both go together. In each other's arms, if you want to. How do you fancy that, Matt? You never did quite get to first base, did you?'

Neither of us spoke. Lindsay's breath was coming in jerky gasps, and just before I spoke again she said:

'Did you send the cops to my flat, that night, Marvin?'

He nodded.

'I planned to get rid of you both then, and clear out right away. Luckily I was delayed.' He chuckled. 'I was annoyed at the time, but when I found out that Grant was missing I was glad that I was still here to keep an eye on things.'

'I never did quite understand how they'd got there,' Lindsay said bitterly. 'You were the last person in my mind.'

I looked from one to the other of them, scarcely hearing what they were saying. That Freeman should have managed to use me for his own ends right to the last didn't surprise me at all, it was the way that Lindsay had betrayed me which hurt the most. In spite of that, though, I was still determined to save her if I could, to give her a chance of getting away from Freeman.

I saw that it wouldn't be long before he fired his two shots, one for each of us. Lindsay glanced towards me, and her expression now was totally different from what it had been. Now, she was begging me to help her, and, whatever I might have thought before, that look would have changed my mind.

I tensed myself to jump, but before I could move there was a sound from the passage.

The we heard a voice.

Calloran's.

★   ★   ★

He came into the room as we turned towards him. He was smiling, and the gun in his hand was slightly bigger than the one which Freeman was holding.

'How did you get in?' Freeman demanded.

'I'm not a fool,' Calloran said. 'If I want to get into a place, I get into it.'

'What made you come here?'

Calloran nodded towards me.

'Grant led my men here,' he said. 'I knew about your connection with Lindsay a long time ago, and after that it was just a matter of adding everything up.' His voice sharpened. 'Where's the money Freeman? My money.'

'I haven't — '

'Where is it?'

I watched the pair of them, trying to see if there was any advantage which I could take. From the moment that Calloran had come into the room

241

Freeman had ceased to take any notice of me, and it would have been easy to get his gun; the real trouble lay with Calloran, who was too experienced to let himself fall into that trap. In any case I didn't know how many of his thugs Calloran had with him; start trouble, and I might find out that there was only one end.

Suddenly, Calloran himself moved, darting forwards, towards Freeman. He clubbed him across the head with his pistol, not hard enough to knock Freeman out, but hard enough to send him staggering across the room. His gun hit the floor with a dull thud. The glass he had been holding followed, smashing, leaving a slowly spreading stain on the carpet.

'Where is it?'

Freeman mumbled something. I couldn't hear the words, but Calloran did and from his expression they weren't an answer to his question.

The end came with startling suddenness.

Lindsay's gaze was fixed on the spot where Freeman's gun had fallen. Without warning she jumped forward, reaching out to snatch it. Calloran half turned. He fired one shot, then another. Lindsay screamed, then fell against one of the chairs, still trying to get the gun. Her fingers had actually closed over it when Calloran fired again.

She jerked once, as the bullet hit her, and then lay still.

While they were both staring at her, I moved. Knowing that if I tried to get the gun I'd be shot too, I didn't bother. All I was concerned about was getting out of the room. As I crossed it, wondering why it hadn't seemed such a long way when I came in, I expected to feel a slug boring into my back, expected each step to be my last, expected anything apart from what actually happened.

I reached the door safely. I even managed to open it, and when I risked a look round I saw why.

Calloran's attention was fully taken up by his battle with Freeman.

Quickly, I padded along the passage, wondering whether or not my theory was right. Usually in this type of house there would be a cellar, and if I'd wanted to hide anything as bulky as forty thousand pounds in small notes, that's the place I'd choose.

The cellar door was at the end of the passage. Wrenching it open I stepped into the darkness, trying to find a light switch, reminded vividly of when I'd fled from Lindsay's flat, just before I'd met up with Sally and Nobby. Briefly I wondered what was happening to them, and Doctor Kyme, of course. Had they tried to work out where I'd gone? Was there any way they could find me now, or would they have to wait until the newspapers came out for the answers to their questions? I wasn't really bothered as long as I found the money; that was now the dominating influence in my mind, blotting out even the fact that Lindsay had been killed.

There was a light switch. I pressed it, and then I knew that I'd been right. At the far side of the white-washed room were three suitcases, stacked neatly against the wall, two pale blue and one green. I started to tremble with excitement as I saw them, and could hardly get over to them fast enough. At last the money which had caused all the trouble was almost within my grasp. I didn't really care what happened now, so long as I didn't come out of things empty handed. I grinned as I got hold of the handle of the top case on the stack, and then two sounds knocked the grin right off my face. The first was another shot.

The second was the unmistakeable sound of a police car siren.

The cops must have been attracted by the noise of the firing. Once they got here we'd all be lost, and it was with feverish haste that I scrabbled at the suitcase, trying to slide it forward, surprised to find that it was so heavy I could barely move it.

Money was never as heavy as that, not even when there was so much crammed into one case. The cases must have been steel lined; that was the only explanation I could think of.

At last, it moved, sliding forward. I let it thud to the floor, choking a little as a cloud of dust rose up. The bang was loud enough to echo round the room, but the edge of the case wasn't even dented. With mounting panic I tried to open it, kicking at it with a force which would easily have burst the locks on a normal case, but which made no impression on this one.

All the while the sound of the siren was getting louder. In my frenzy I tried the other two cases, both as heavy as the first, both equally impossible to get open. The dawning realization that I wasn't going to get any of the money at all almost made me physically sick, but then I had other problems.

The sound of the siren, after reaching a new height of loudness, stopped abruptly, and the deathly silence which followed was broken by the sound of a car door slamming.

They were here! If I was going to get away I'd have to forget the money, forget everything except what I was doing now, and where the cops were likely to be. With a last glance at the suitcases I ran up the stone steps, back into the passage and into the lounge.

Calloran was on the floor near Lindsay, lying still, blood welling slowly from his arm. At the far side, Freeman was holding his gun, the tip of his tongue curling out of his mouth, trying to stop the flow of blood from his upper lip. By the time he saw me it was too late and I was already launched towards him. The full pent up fury of the past few months went into the blow I gave him, and with a faint scream he fell sideways, his flailing arm smashing the glass front of the drinks cabinet.

'That's for me, Marvin,' I said, then, as he lay there, I kicked at him savagely until he stopped moving. 'And those are for Lindsay,' I told him, though I doubt whether he heard me.

The cops were ringing at the bell. In front of me, the window offered a convenient way out. I looked round, at Lindsay, dead, at Freeman, unconscious, and Calloran still bleeding, then I leaned over and opened the window. With any luck the cops would have their hands full looking into Calloran's affairs, and wouldn't have much time left to bother about me.

All I'd have to worry about would be Cranston.

That was plenty.

I scrambled out of the window, hurried as silently as I could across the garden, avoiding the part where the lights of the Panda car made a bright splash, picking out the bushes, with tangled leaves and branches showing darkly against the brightness, and hopped over the wall into a quiet side street.

There were no cops around now.

All I had to do then was walk away, back into my lonely life.

THE END

We do hope that you have enjoyed reading this large print book.

Did you know that all of our titles are available for purchase?

We publish a wide range of high quality large print books including:
Romances, Mysteries, Classics
General Fiction
Non Fiction and Westerns

Special interest titles available in large print are:
The Little Oxford Dictionary
Music Book, Song Book
Hymn Book, Service Book

Also available from us courtesy of Oxford University Press:
Young Readers' Dictionary
(large print edition)
Young Readers' Thesaurus
(large print edition)

For further information or a free brochure, please contact us at:
Ulverscroft Large Print Books Ltd.,
The Green, Bradgate Road, Anstey,
Leicester, LE7 7FU, England.
Tel: (00 44) **0116 236 4325**
Fax: (00 44) **0116 234 0205**

DEADLY JIGSAW

Roger Bay

Fighting his way out of the closing net is Adam Kane, chief investigator for a large Insurance Company in Australia . . . Hot on the trail of a million dollar swindle Kane comes up against the Big Boy, a master criminal, and two of his deadly killers . . . The chase, with Kane being the hunted instead of the hunter, moves swiftly from Australia to Fiji, then down to the hot thermal pools of New Zealand before the last piece of the jigsaw is put into place.